Welcome to the Working Week

Welcome
to the
Working Week

Paul Vlitos

First published in Great Britain in 2007 by Orion Books,
an imprint of The Orion Publishing Group Ltd
Orion House, 5 Upper Saint Martin's Lane
London, WC2H 9EA
An Hachette Livre UK Company

10 9 8 7 6 5 4 3 2 1

A CIP catalogue record for this book is available
from the British Library.

ISBN (Hardback): 978 0 7528 8511 7
ISBN (Trade paperback): 978 0 7528 8512 4

Typeset by Deltatype Ltd, Birkenhead, Merseyside

Printed and bound at Mackays of Chatham plc,
Chatham, Kent

The Orion Publishing Group's policy is to use papers that
are natural, renewable and recyclable products and made
from wood grown in sustainable forests. The logging and
manufacturing processes are expected to conform to the
environmental regulations of the country of origin.

www.orionbooks.co.uk

Acknowledgements

For their advice and encouragement at various points I'd like to thank Cara Jennings, Katy Vlitos, my parents, Jenny McGrath, Julia Jordan, David McAllister, Alex von Tunzelmann, Claire Sargent, Heather Tilley, Nick Jones, Louise Joy, James Martin and Oliver Seares.

Very special thanks also to my agent Gráinne Fox, and to Genevieve Pegg, Jon Wood and the team at Orion Books.

Part One
The Offer of a Lifetime

Martin • A Jesus-shaped Hole

The Moustache • Barney

Friends Reunited

Potential Flatmates

Sally and David

Batsard

On Sunday at 18:56 Kate Staple wrote:

Dear Martin the Batsard,

I am sending you this at your work account because I know your bitch girlfriend reads your hotmail one and unlike some people I have dignity. I just got your answering phone message. HOW DARE YOU? I knew you were a coward but I never knew how much of a coward you were until now (when I got your message). I am disgusted with you and with myself. Martin you make me sick.

REPLY TO ME.

Love, Kate

p.s. I think I have a disease and I sincerely hope you (and your girlfriend) have it too.

p.p.s. By the way, I did assume you were gay when I met you. So did my friends.

On Monday at 10:07 Kate Staple wrote:

Dear Martin,

Why have you not replied to me? Are you REALLY such a coward? I haven't slept at all (well one hour). I am very upset with you. I'm sorry about what I wrote about your girlfriend. I really need to hear from you. I'm at work now, but I'm checking my hotmail. Please reply to me.

Love, Kate

Dear Kate

Sorry not to reply to you sooner, I was a little late into work this morning due to a bomb scare at Baker Street. I've just got round to reading your messages. I think you meant to send them to Martin Sergeant, who works in the IT department. His email is ms23@mediasolutions.com. I am the other Martin Sargent, ms24@mediasolutions.com. It is a common mistake! Please don't worry about it. I hope you and Martin reach an amicable agreement.
Best Wishes
Martin Sargent

P.S. I'm sorry to hear about your disease.
P.P.S. We all assumed Martin was gay at first as well. I think it's those glasses.

Offer of a Lifetime

On Monday at 13:32 Martin Sargent wrote:

Hello all

Due to an unforeseen domestic rearrangement, there is a room available to rent if anyone is interested. If you are looking for a place to live (or know someone who is) please get in touch. This should not be taken as an excuse to offload your undesirable flatmate/lover on me. The details are as follows:

The flat: damp, mysterious odour, dark. Close to train line. Enigmatic boiler provides tepid water almost on demand.

The location: Kensal Green, NW 11 (Zone 2)

Why not take advantage of a limited period offer to experience this part of London before it's gentrified?

A twenty-minute walk to the tube takes you past the local amenities: closed public baths, semi-closed library (wide selection of work-out DVDs and large-print books), over-priced 24-hour shop, crap video shop, one halal butcher's, two dodgy pubs, one shiny new curry palace, 4 posters about gun crime, 3 appeals for witnesses.

Experience the vibrant multiculturalism of contemporary London at first hand. Listen as the schoolkids banter playfully with Mr Singh, our local shopkeeper. See them pocket Twix bars when he isn't looking. Shrug as they stare you out. Hear domestic disputes in five mellifluous languages. Smile with pride as our local lads comment appreciatively on your bike. Meet our fashionably diverse local crew of derelicts. There is also some brilliant if baffling graffiti: 'Love is for Suckers', 'I Hate Your Dog' and 'Sit on it' are my personal favourites.

Celebrity local residents include Isambard Kingdom Brunel, celebrity chef Alexis Soyer and Anthony Trollope. Apart from the world-famous cemetery, Kensal Green shops also boasts one of London's few surviving Victorian public toilets, featuring elegant tiling and a tasteful pseudo-classical portico. Make use of it now before it is converted into a desirable flat.

Don't delay. Every month the health-food shops and gastropubs of Queen's Park are creeping west. The first skips of spring have appeared in the road already. Soon the sights, smells, and noises of this lively part of London will be transformed for ever.

The occupant: moody, newly single smoker, 25. Dislikes job. No hobbies. Casual about housework. But not too casual...

Should interest: sociologist looking for area-study; exiled dictator looking for somewhere quiet to hide out; language student; trainspotter; graffitologist.

Please do not apply if any of the following words describes you: zany; bubbly; fussy; spiritual; kleptomaniac.

Rent: extortionate.

I anticipate great demand, so please pass the word around without delay.

Martin

A Jesus-shaped Hole

On Monday at 13:05 Martin Sargent wrote:

Hi Mum

Writing to say thanks for the parcel. I think the jumper is actually Dad's, but tell him I'll take good care of it. The book looks very interesting, and I look forward to getting the chance to read it. Hope is all well with you. I'm not sure about the weekend yet.

Lots of Love

Martin

On Monday at 13:10 Martin Sargent wrote:

Hey Sis

Hope term is going OK, and that life in Hall is still treating you well. I take it you're getting leaned on to go home this weekend as well? On the subject of which, I got the most extraordinary parcel from the Mum this morning. She sent me one of Dad's jumpers (that piece of foolery with the leather elbow-pads that makes him look like a retired general) under the insane misapprehension that it belongs to me. I also got a book titled *Is There a Jesus-shaped Hole in Your Life?*. I wasn't aware of it, though I am strongly conscious of a Sally-shaped hole in my love-life and a TV-and-video-shaped hole in my living room. On which note, do mention to that next-door neighbour of yours that I am now single. Speak tonight about weekend?

Love

Martin

P.S. I'm thinking of growing a moustache. Any suggestions for shape?

On Tuesday at 00:25 Lucy Sargent replied:

Hi, Martin,

In computer room at college, checking messages after night out. Mmm, chips are good. Very sorry again to hear about you and Sally (and about your TV). Next-door neighbour is here (her name is Miriam, by the way) and says Hi, but I think she has a boyfriend. Also, don't be a perve. Thought you were supposed to be heartbroken?

So I guess we won't speak tonight about weekend, but I think I may make an appearance on Sunday. Surprising how fast an allowance can go, isn't it? Last time I saw that jumper Lady was sleeping on it, so I would give it a wash if I was you.

Love,
Lucy

PS: I would advise against moustache of any description. Miriam agrees. How about a Jesus-shaped beard? (Shape of Jesus' beard, not beard in shape of Messiah obviously.) Will await further developments, and maybe see you at weekend?

On Thursday at 13:57 Martin Sargent wrote:

Hi Sis

Dad rang last night, so clearly there is a three-line whip as regards Sunday's family festivities. I'm still not quite clear why this weekend of all possible weekends we have to gather the clan. It's not that I have anything better lined up, more that almost anything else I can think of to do would be more fun than being at home. Apparently there's a big pile of my old shirts waiting for me to go through them and decide which ones I want to keep and which ones can go to the jumble. To be perfectly honest, since I haven't worn a single one of those shirts for almost a decade, I probably wouldn't have missed any of them. I'm also unconvinced that it's a giant parental vote of confidence in me that they have kept my Sainsbury's uniform 'in case I need it again'.

I told Dad I'll be down Saturday morning, but I'll have to get away sharpish after lunch on Sunday. Sally's coming round Sunday evening to return some things she has decided she doesn't want and to steal some more of my stuff. I hope you've recovered from Monday night, and I'm sorry to hear that Miriam has a boyfriend. Is he better-looking than me? Is he taller? Is he tougher?

Wow, that book Mum gave me has really changed my life. I will give it to you at the weekend. I have abandoned the moustache idea and decided to give my life to God. As most of my worldly possessions are now in Sally's new flat, I'm already at an advantage as regards renouncing them. I have decided to forgive everyone. Can't wait to tell Mum the good news.

Love

Martin

On Friday at 16:52 Lucy Sargent replied:

Dear St Martin,

Yeah, right, you gaylord.

By the way, I met Miriam's boyfriend Frank last night (and over breakfast). As he is a large rugby-playing man, I would avoid tangling with him. Although, interestingly, he has a beard. The shape of it defies description somewhat, as it's hard to tell where the beard ends and the neck acne begins. Rather perverse I would have thought to have a beard AND shaving rash. Not a look I recommend you go for.

See you Saturday – presumably this means you'll be accompanying Mum to church on Sunday?

Love,

Lucy

David

On Monday at 11:35 Martin Sargent wrote:

Hi Lucy

Good to see you at the weekend. Very kind of you to suggest I wear my 'new' jumper to church on Sunday. And I still maintain the vicar was sniggering at my stupid elbow-pads. Possibly because I kept slipping off the communion rail.

Well, the plot thickens with Sally. As expected she turned up to pick up a few (more) things - she rather absurdly accused me of hoarding some of her underwear (which I hadn't, of course).

Not that she turned up alone. Her friend David gave her a lift over. Very kind of him. You may remember him from Sally's and my last party (which I didn't realise at the time would be our *last* party). He was ambushing people in the hall and handing out flyers for his play. As I recall he was outfitted in tapered combat trousers, a white shirt and a waistcoat Ali Baba would have rejected as being a bit 'busy'. He ends, abruptly, about five feet from the ground, in an explosion of ginger hair. Like a rather disappointing firework. I didn't see his car, but I imagine it looking like the Noddymobile.

This is NOT how it happens. I don't get dumped for David. David is the guy who gets dumped at the end when Sally realises who she really loves. He ends up falling in a duck-pond or getting a ton of manure dumped on him. He could be played by Tom Hollander in a ginger wig.

Mild revenge: I managed to slip *Is There a Jesus-Shaped Hole in Your Life?* into a box of books I was helping pack for Sally.

She sends her love, by the way.

Love

Martin

10

On Monday at 12:45 Lucy Sargent replied:

Poor Martin!

So sorry to hear about all that. I do recall David. Physically, he's more how Mackenzie Crook would look playing Malcolm McLaren. But that's not his fault. We discussed his life and works at length in the hall while he tried to peer down my top. Alas for him he was too short and he's not really my type. On the subject of casting, he told me I had the perfect face to play Lizzie Bennet in *Pride and Prejudice*. He'd make a great Mr Collins. Are you sure Sally and he are a thing? Perhaps he has hypnotic powers. Or perhaps you really pissed her off ...

The jumper looked pretty good, actually. We discovered you had accidentally left it after I dropped you at the station. In fact, you'd left it right at the back of your cupboard, stuffed behind a bag full of plastic dinosaurs. It was very lucky for you that Mum found it. Auntie Jean came round and we were looking for your school photo.

Take care of yourself, and for god's sake shave that monstrosity on your top lip off before you see Sally again. Send her my regards when you see her.

    Love,
    Lucy

PS: Someone was insisting to me the other day that ginger is the new blonde. I can't remember who it was now. Possibly Mick Hucknall.

Moustache

On Monday at 17:58 Elizabeth Sargent wrote:

Hi, Martin,

Hope things went well (or at least as well as they could in
the circumstances) with Sally last night. We found after you
had gone that you had left your jumper! Will send it on. I
don't suppose you want your old plastic dinosaurs. By the way,
whatever happened to your old school photo? I wanted to show
it to Auntie Jean. I'll look forward to hearing what you *really*
thought of the book. Make sure to look after yourself. Life goes
on, you know.

Love,

Mum

PS: Sorry to have to tell you but Lady has cancer again.

PPS: Darling, you know that wherever you go and whatever you
do your father and I will always love and support you. But
we do think that moustache is something of an error.

Offer of a Lifetime

On Tuesday at 9:54 Barney wrote:

Alright mate,

Long time and all that. Got your email about the flat. Afraid I am already installed with Uni mates in Balham. Not sure if you knew I was in London? Quite a few of the guys from school live around here actually. Shall I see if any of them are looking to move? Flat sounds pretty attractive. As for the company... That's you, right? Doesn't sound like you have changed much from school (except you weren't 25 at school). By the way, it might be worth thinking about making the advert more positive if you are serious about getting someone to move in.

It would be good to meet up, wouldn't it? Give me a ring (mobile still the same) if you are free over the weekend.

By the way, if you are free Saturday, I'm DJing in a bar up your way. I'll put you on the guestlist if you fancy it. Would be good to get a few friendly faces in the crowd... (Details attached)

Laters, Maters,

Barney

Saturdays @ Bar Loco
'It's Loco Time!'
15 Victoria Street
Tube: Royal Oak/Warwick Avenue
Pitchers £7.50 till 10   Shooters £3
After 7.30: £5 on the door; £4 w/flyer
No Trainers
Sounds by DJ Barney

On Tuesday at 10:15 Sally wrote:

Dear Martin,
I don't think you meant to include me on that mailing-list?
Good luck with finding someone quickly. I have put the cheque
for last month's electricity in the post. It was nice to see you the
other day. Hope things OK with you. Speak soon, Perhaps we
could go out for a drink sometime?
Warmest regards,
Sally

On Tuesday at 10:17 Martin wrote:

Dear Sally
No, I meant to put you on the list. Thanks for sending the
cheque on. I miss you. As regards that pint, an old mate is DJing
at a bar not far from me on Saturday - he's offered to put us on
the guestlist. It's Barney from school, but the bar's alright.
Love
Martin

P.S. 'Warmest regards'?!?!?

At 16:59 on Tuesday Sally replied:

Dear Martin,
Sounds great! I'll have to come straight from rehearsal. Do
you think you could put David on the list as well? I'm glad things
are cool between us. See you then.
Lots of love
Sally

PS - By the way, David really likes the moustache. If that's what
that thing is supposed to be.

Re: Offer of a Lifetime

At 11:21 on Friday Martin Sergeant wrote:

Dear Martin (!),

Hi, this is Martin Sergeant (in IT). Rumour has it you're looking for a flatmate? I was wondering if you could send me the details? I've recently started looking for somewhere to live myself, so perhaps if I catch you at lunch we could discuss it?

Best,

Martin Sergeant (not you!!!)

At 11:37 on Friday Martin Sargent replied:

Hi Martin

Not sure yet, but I think the room might be taken. Thanks for your interest, look forward to discussing it with you.

See you at lunch

Martin

At 11:40 on Friday Martin Sargent wrote:

Hi Laura

How's things down in production? Don't suppose you know who's been spreading the word that I'm looking for a housemate? More to the point, how does Martin Sargent know about it? I just wondered if you had mentioned it. Otherwise, I wonder whether he is monitoring my emails? In which case, 'Hi Martin'. Want to go out (for sandwiches) this lunchtime?

Still no luck finding anyone to move in, by the way...

Let me know about lunch.
Martin

At 11:52 on Friday Laura replied:

Martin,
No idea how the other MS heard about it, since I hadn't heard.
Slightly hurt, in fact, that you didn't ask me. I have a 'working'
'lunch', so looks like fish and chips with your namesake for you.
By the way, if you're so desperate for a housemate, what's wrong
with Martin? I trust it's not prejudice.
　　Soon,

　　　　　　　　　　　　　Laura

At 12:04 on Friday Martin replied:

Laura
You will note I topped your flirty 12-minute response time
with a nonchalant 14 minutes. My reasons for not wanting
to live with Martin have nothing to do with his orientation
(he's not, by the way). Firstly, I have it on good authority he
is a batsard, and may well be diseased (in an unspecific but
unpleasant way). Second, I don't want to live with anyone from
work. Third, he is the kind of person who reads magazines. And
not on the train.
　　Of course, I thought of you as a flatmate immediately. But: 1)
See reason two above, and 2) I may have other plans for you.
How soon?
Martin

At 14:45 on Friday Laura replied:

Martin,
Two hours and forty-one minutes. Beat that! Look forward to

hearing about your battered cod with Martin. Also about your surprising grasp of his medical history.

'Other plans' sounds a bit sinister. Free this weekend.

Laura

At 16:55 on Friday Martin replied:

Laura

Only two hours ten, but it's time to go home. Genuinely busy this weekend. You're obviously a popular girl.

Have a good one.

Martin

P.S. I'm very heartbroken and vulnerable at the moment.

At 16:59 on Friday Laura replied:

Yes, I heard about the break-up. I'm sorry about that, and it's obviously very sad, but can I ask one question? Were her parting words 'Either me or that moustache has to go?' If they were I'm afraid to say I think you may have made the wrong choice.

At 17:02 on Friday Martin replied:

OK, OK, I get the message. I fact I got the message last night when a gang of kids behind me on the bus started singing 'macho, macho man.' I suspect they were being ironic.

Re: David

On Sunday at 18:34 Barney wrote:

Alright Mate,

Thanks for coming last night. I hope you had a good time. It was good of so many people to turn up. Sorry about the muck-up with the guestlist. I'd love to know what you thought of my set. They cut me a bit short, actually, and they were a bit funny about some of the stuff I played, but everyone I spoke to was really encouraging.

I was wondering if you could let me have your mate David's email? We were talking about my maybe doing the music for a play he's directing, and I wanted to follow it up. He seems like a really chilled guy.

Cheers, Ears,

Barney

Jumper

On Tuesday at 11:15 Martin wrote:

Hey Luce

It turns out the joke is on me. I went to see Barney from school DJing at a bar on Saturday and about three people were wearing the exact same jumper as the one Mum keeps sending me. It seems to be some Paddy-Ashdown-chic thing.

You probably remember Barney (Mark Barnwell). He used to have a floppy fringe and wear a pinstriped jacket to parties. He's about eight feet high with a chin like the prow of a trireme. Well, if you want to hear some crap music ineptly cued, book him for an event. I will never be able to erase from my memory the image of him pumping his fist in the air, with a grin on his face as if he is jamming onstage with Miles Davis, when he's actually playing a mix of ironic hits to a bunch of idiots from school in a bar with no dancefloor. Not one of the greatest evenings ever. Although, having said that, David obviously enjoyed it. Indeed, they are thinking of an artistic collaboration. In a better-organised society those two would be stoned to the edge of town and banished into the desert.

Various schoolies were lurking around appraising each other. I had an extraordinary conversation with one Philip Hayward. In a brief pause in the music (Barney managed to unplug himself by dancing around behind the decks) Hayward managed to drop into conversation three times that he was 'not academically brilliant'. He emphasised the 'academically', and there wasn't much I could do except nod politely and clutch my five-quid pint to my chest to avoid it being bashed out of my hands by the coke-fuelled harpies and posh thugs struggling to get to the bar. I got the strong impression, though, that I was being asked to vouch

19

for having recognised some special quality in him, even as a boy. The whole thing was a bit baffling.

He used to be in my history set, and I don't remember him being spectacularly stupid, but then I don't remember much about him at all, except that he fell in a river on the last day of school (or was he pushed?). Anyway, it was clearly his impression that I spend a great deal of time lying awake and thinking about how stupid he was (or is). I didn't quite catch in what way he was hinting that he was so very brilliant that society had neglected to notice. I kept expecting him to tell me he knew how to make a boat, or a pot, but he didn't. He hasn't made a million since school, or invented a cure for anything, or done much of anything I can tell except go to university and move to Clapham to live with old schoolfriends. He doesn't make clothes, or music, or even jokes. So in what way his implicit brilliance might ever be measured is hard to tell. I think he reviews restaurants online. And he was wearing Dad's jumper. All of which reminds me why I ceremonially set fire to my school photo before going off to uni. I won't tell you how I put it out.

Anyway, too long already this email, so I will say goodbye. Hope all well with you.

Love

Martin

P.S. Philip did mention, though, that he has a mate from college called Ross who is looking for somewhere to live, and he has promised to put us in touch. The mind boggles at what I'm letting myself in for there...

On Wednesday at 12:15 Lucy replied:

Hi, Martin,

Sounds pretty ghastly. Of course I remember Barney. I used to think he was pretty fit, actually, although I see what you mean about the trireme chin. Didn't quite follow for a minute and thought you meant he has enormous painted eyes on the side of his head (has he?).

I don't suppose your irritation with Philip Hayward has anything to do with your email's conspicuous failure to mention Sally?

How is the work flirtation coming on?

Love,

Lucy

PS: Oh *that* was why you burned the school photo. I'd forgotten that. But then I was under the impression you burned it because it you looked like a freak in it.

PPS: To be fair, you did look like a freak in it.

On Wednesday at 14:15 Martin replied:

Hey Luce

I had lunch with the divine Laura today, as it happens. I doubt it will go anywhere, but it's certainly better than having lunch with Martin Sergeant (don't ask). I was enthralled to learn that she doesn't write, or paint, or act, or DJ. She will no doubt turn out to do all of the above.

As for Sally, she of course looked stunning on Saturday and was polite and charming and generally winning. She even found ways to compliment Barney (I was cornered and made to confess my opinion too: I managed 'interesting'). Which left me in an undefined and generally foul mood, which the next day drifted seamlessly into a hideous hangover. I paid a man in the loos a quid for watching me have a slash and dispensing some soap. At first I felt noble, then I felt exploited, then I realised how much the cab home alone would be and almost asked for my money back. I believe I made a drunken effort to persuade Sally to come back with me, which largely consisted of saying things like 'You're amazing; the flat is a mess without you.' I was under the impression I had said 'My life is a mess.' Needless to say, she left with David.

By the way, I notice you are cultivating an undergraduate attitude of barbed insight. Very impressive, but I do miss the old air of unqualified admiration.

Love

Martin

P.S. Too late, I realise that I should have told Barney his set reminded me of seeing Fatboy Slim play Brighton Beach. He would have been thrilled, and I wouldn't have mentioned that the specific aspect of that experience which came to mind was point at which to my horror I saw a middle-aged raver taking a crap in the sea. There was something about Barney DJing that reminded me of the mixture of pleasure and anxiety on that man's face.

P.P.S. I only looked like a freak in the school picture because they made us line up alphabetically, and I was stuck between Mark 'Basher' Townsend and Andreas 'Andy the Dandy' Sedgeworth. I looked like the middle figure in the ascent of man. Or a composite photograph out of a Victorian study of degenerate types.

On Wednesday at 16:42 Lucy replied:

Oh dear, sounds like you played it pretty uncool with Sally. As for 'unqualified admiration', that may have always been in your head, I'm afraid.

Love,

Lucy

PS: Whatever happened to 'Andy the Dandy'? He was a living legend at my school. Girls used to weep openly at the thought of his perfect centre parting.

Yes, Andy used to use a ruler for that. It took him hours.
Tragically, it turned out not to be a transferable skill. He was
back living at home, the last I heard. However, I believe he is still
a living legend at your school. No doubt the police are gathering
a dossier as we speak.

On Wednesday at 16:46 Lucy replied:

'Here, Sarge, we've managed to dig out the suspect's old school
photo. Christ, look at this geezer next to him. Looks like the love-
child of Mr Bean and Sawney Bean. Do you think it's a ring?
Let's drag him in and see what he has to say for himself.'

Take care, and let me know how things go with the
mysterious Laura. By the way, we haven't heard much about
your book recently ...

Re: Re: Offer of a Lifetime

On Sunday at 19:27 Crazylegs75 wrote:

Hi Martin,
A friend of yours forwarded your message to me. Are you still looking for a housemate?
I am: fun, flirty female twenty-something (just!).
I love: dancing, clubs, music.
Sounds like you're spending too much time in the flat alone. If you pick me as your new housemate I promise to make your life 200 percent more fun. I'm not too fussy about housework either.
Working in boring job at the moment, but do a bit of dancing as well (club, and a bit of freelance pole/lap).
Look forward to hearing from you
    Love
    Susan.

On Monday at 15:45 Martin replied:

Dear 'Crazylegs'
Sorry for the delay in getting back to you. I'm afraid my account dumped your message in with the junkmail. Thank you very much for your kind offer to increase my fun levels by 200%. I take it the friend who gave you my email address was Barney? I am afraid that the room is already taken.
Regretfully
Martin

On Tuesday at 12:30 Barney wrote:

Hey Mate,

I'm following up on my request for David's email? Sorry to bother you again, but it would be great to contact him before the end of the day.

By the way, did my mate Suzie email you? If you're looking for a flatmate she's incredible. Really amazing energy levels - and not only on the dancefloor!!! Seriously though, she'd be pretty great to live with, if you think you could handle it. She'd transform your flat into party central, mate! Let me know what you think of the idea...

Cheers in advance for David's email address,

See Ya Soon, Loon,

Barney

On Tuesday at 12:40 Martin replied:

Barney

I don't have David's email. Why don't you see if it's on his webpage. If you google 'theatre' + 'London' + 'loathsome pretentious diminutive girlfriend thief' you'll probably find his site. It lists every possible way of contacting him. No doubt he's also on MySpace. I think you'd make a very good team, so would advise you to go for it.

As regards your mate Crazylegs75, I got a very excitable email from her enquiring about the place. Not entirely sure we're temperamentally compatible, I'm afraid. As I mentioned to her, I think I have someone ready to take the room, and I don't really want to muck them about etc. etc. I'm sure you'll pass on my apologies. If she's looking for a place to live, perhaps suggest the Big Brother house...

But thanks for passing the word around. As I mentioned, I think the place is taken, so no need to go to any more effort. Cheers though.

Martin

On Tuesday at 20:52 MadMan22 wrote:

Hi, Mart,
Barney passed on the word that you have a room. Any space for another 'smoker'? I have some cutlery and other accessories. Working in a tattoo parlour in Camden at the moment. Could arrange a deal if you need anything inked or pierced. How convenient are you for the Northern Line? Barney was telling me some good things about you, mate. Think this could be the start of something wicked ...
Let me know about the room,
Adrian

On Wednesday at 9:28 Martin replied:

Hello Adrian
Thanks for yours. Very inconvenient for the Northern Line, I'm afraid. Also, I have someone interested in the room. Sorry about that.
Good luck with the room-search.
Martin

On Wednesday at 9:45 Sam Hucks wrote:

Martin,
Huckster here. Need accommodation. I been away for a while. Questions: Do you cook? Do you clean? Are you flexible about rent?
If so, I'll take it.
THE HUCKSTER

On Wednesday at 10:00 Martin replied:

No, No, No, and No you won't.
Martin

On Wednesday at 10:17 LadySpank wrote:

Hi Martin,
Word is you have a room. I'd love to take it. I hope the room is still available. I heard about you and the housework. Sounds like you are a pretty dirty boy. I warn you, as housemates go I am pretty dominant! I hope you don't mind me working from home at the weekends.
Love
Lady Spank

On Wednesday at 10:19 Martin replied:

Oh sod off, Barney. Haven't you got anything better to do?
Warm Regards
Martin

Blocking Unwanted Email

On Wednesday at 14:03 Martin Sargent wrote:

Hi Martin

Nice to see you for lunch the other day. Hope we can do it again soon, and I hope you find somewhere to live soon too. This is a work-related email (for once!): Is it possible to block email from the same sender, if they are using different names?

Many thanks

Martin

On Wednesday at 16:57 Martin Sergeant wrote:

Hi, mate

Yeah, no problem. In fact, there's a few things we can do to improve your email set-up generally. I'll pop up tomorrow morning. Most people are using the newer, much improved system we've been installing around the building, so I'll set you up with that at the same time. It's a lot more streamlined and about 150 % faster, as well as giving you a much wider range of available functions.

       Martin

On Wednesday at 17:02 Martin Sargent wrote:

Cheers, mate

Really appreciate the rapid response, by the way. If it's all the same, I'm quite happy with the rest of the computer as it is, but

appreciate your offer. See you tomorrow.
Martin

On Thursday at 11:56 Martin Sargent wrote:

Dear Martin@helpdesk
Sorry to bother you again, but it seems like I've been blocked
from getting online entirely. Would be great if you could have a
look at my account.
Cheers
Martin

On Thursday at 12:01 Martin Sargent wrote:

Bloody IT! I asked Martin to do one little thing, but he
insisted on rejigging the whole computer brain and now it's gone
mental (technical terms). Are you using this allegedly 'improved'
system? It lets me do a million new things I don't want to do, but
it won't let me send external email or go online. I can't even find
my inbox any more. I am sending this out in the vague hope it
will get to you... Not holding my breath.

On Thursday at 12:10 Laura replied:

Got it! You see, it does work. I can't believe you were still on
the old system. Wasn't it really slow?

On Thursday at 12:15 Martin replied:

It was slow, but at least I knew how to use it. This is
ridiculous. If I don't get the internet back soon I will have to
do some work. Why does IT always do that? I don't need to
downline movies or upstream an ipod, I just want to be able to

find emails people have sent me. It's like you go to the garage to get your wing-mirror fixed and they install a rocket engine. One that doesn't work. Better go, this is turning into bad stand-up.

Shall I download sandwiches for two in about an hour?

On Thursday at 16:58 Martin Sargent wrote:

Dear Martin@helpdesk
Sorry, it's me again. Any chance of getting my external email/internet access back?
Thanks again
Martin

On Friday at 9:24 Martin Sargent wrote:

Dear Martin@helpdesk
Help! I think the entire internet has disappeared. Perhaps it has been kidnapped and is being held to ransom. Either that, or you have buggered up something on my computer. In either case, please sort it out when you get a chance.
Cheers
Martin

P.S. Although I am really starting to get into solitaire.

On Friday at 10:11 Martin Sargent wrote:

Hi Martin@'help'desk
I know you're really busy, but I kind of need my external email to do any work. Any possibility of getting it back today?
Thanks and sorry again
Martin

On Friday at 12:15 Martin Sargent wrote:

Dear Martin@helpdesk

I have some questions I hope you can help me with:

- Is it acceptable to wear brown shoes at a formal event?

- I occasionally suffer mild irritation when I shave. Should I change my moisturising routine?

- Whose coronation is celebrated by the coronation chicken sandwich? And why do they have those horrible puffy raisins in them?

- Can you suggest any healthy alternatives to dairy?

- Why is it called Echo Beach, if waves make the only sound?

I'm asking on the off chance that for all this time I have fundamentally misunderstood the kind of 'help' your 'desk' is supposed to provide.

Oh, also I am having trouble with my computer.

Martin

On Friday at 15:45 Martin Sargent wrote:

Checking on the email/internet situation again. Any chance of getting it fixed over the weekend?

Have a good one.

Martin

On Monday at 9:13 Martin Sargent wrote:

Hi Laura

I've finally got the internet back. I think I am the object of a vendetta. Martin S isn't replying to me and I had to go to the IT cave four times before I got someone to come up. And he keeps giving me the thousand-yard stare when I see him in the corridor. I think he's really pissed off about the flat. Hope you had a good weekend?

Martin

On Monday at 9:16 Laura replied:

Hi, Martin,
It may be to do with the fact that I let slip to a few people that he is a cheating 'batsard'. Oops! Unless he really is reading your emails. Weekend dreary.

Laura

On Monday at 9:19 Martin replied:

Oh, well that explains it. I just got a stern email from the IT department about proper use of the internet - cruel irony, since for about a week I have been unable to access it due to their pointless overcompetence. Now I have a stupid backlog of work to catch up with. Lunch tomorrow instead?
Martin

On Monday at 10:12 Ross wrote:

Hi Martin,
I've tried this address a couple of times, but things keep getting returned. Are you having trouble with your email? Philip Hayward mentioned to me that you have a spare room and are looking for someone to fill it. If it's still available it would be great if you could get back to me and we could discuss rent etc. I'd be looking to move in as soon as is convenient for you. Let me know if there's a good time this week for me to pop over and have a look at the flat - and at the same time we can establish that neither of us is a total freak.
Best,

Ross

Re: Re: David

Hello, Martin,

I hope all is well with you. I don't think you are going to be pleased to hear this, but anyway ... Since I've been working with David we've got really close, and it seems silly that since we're spending so much time together rehearsing we are living at other ends of town. Since we're both looking for a place, we are going to move in together at the end of next week. Please don't jump to any conclusions, and don't take things personally (as always). It's a purely practical thing. I've been talking to David a lot about you, and you may be surprised to hear it, but he has been taking your side a lot. As he says, though, sometimes people do simply grow apart, and I think that is what happened between us. I wish you all the best with your writing, of which I have always been tremendously supportive. I still love you a great deal, I am just not in love with you. I hope you are not too hurt, and that you find someone to move into the spare room quickly.

Lots of love,

Sally

On Tuesday at 9:01 Martin replied:

Sally

Thanks for yours. As it happens I have had heaps of interest in the flat, thanks for asking. Good luck with your move. I haven't been writing much, because you took all the pens. I'm never quite sure what people mean by the 'love you/ in love'

divide, but it was nice of you to express concern that I am not 'too' hurt. I suppose a mild amount of pain is acceptable.
See you soon.
Martin

Lady

On Tuesday at 13:45 Elizabeth Sargent wrote:

Dear Martin,

Glad to be able to tell you that Lady seems not to be suffering, although it looks like this time she will have to be put down. By the way, I haven't heard what you thought about the book yet.

Love,

Mum

Part Two
A Face to Watch

Invitation

On Saturday at 14:23 Frequent Flyer Promotions wrote:

Dear All,

Frequent Flyer Promotions presents

Uhe LADY of SHALOTT

Written, Directed and Produced by David Fauntleroy

Starring
Sally Kendle as The Lady of Shalott/Sarah
Mark Thornhill as Lancelot/Lance
Sebastian Tilly as The Mirror/Narrator

Inspired by the poem by Alfred, Lord Tennyson
Soundscapes by DJ Barney.
At The New Place (Over the Two Tuns Inn, SW1)

Brought radically up-to-date, this is an in-your-face 21st century version of the classic Victorian poem. 'Camelot' is the city's hottest nightclub, 'The Lady' is Sarah, a girl coming of age fast in a world of slippery values, who hears from afar about 'Lance', the city's hottest new DJ. Based partly on improvisations developed by the cast and its noted young director, Uhe LADY of SHALOTT will guarantee that you will never think the same way about Victorian love poetry again. Sumptuously staged in the intimate surroundings of The New Place, Uhe LADY of SHALOTT features a mixture of classical music and the latest underground sounds from DJ Barney.

About The Director

David Fauntleroy is fast acquiring a reputation for daring reinterpretations of classic texts. Last year his drum'n'bass *Tristan and Isolde* was acclaimed at the Edinburgh Fringe. While still at university the *Cambridge Evening Post* included him as one of its 'Young Faces to Watch'. With his emphasis on improvisation and reckless experimentation, David Fauntleroy is fast gaining a reputation as one of the most daring new directors now working.

On Monday at 9:15 Martin wrote:

Dear Sally
I got the flyer for the new play. It sounds very interesting. I hope the rehearsals are going well. Look forward to seeing it. Hope you are well.
Martin

On Monday at 9:27 Martin wrote:

Hey Luce
Oh my goddy god. I've attached the flyer for this thing Sally and David have dreamed up. David's surname is Fauntleroy. I believe the idiocies of the play speak for themselves, but may I draw your attention to the following? I like the bit where David claims to have written *The Lady of Shalott*. 'Noted' 'young' director - noted by the *Cambridge Evening Post*, and a 'young' 36. The most 'daring' director now working? I think that is a misspelling for 'shameless'. Unless 'daring' means 'utterly lacking in a sense of the ridiculous and willing to crucify acquaintances with boredom to enhance his own self-esteem'. I notice the blurb fails to mention his shit hair. I'm sorry to have missed the drum'n'bass *Tristan and Isolde*. No doubt the 'Skiffle *Two Gentlemen of Verona*' and the 'Punk *Three Men in a Boat*' were considered pretty radical in their day too. But really, what is the fucking point? I have no doubt theatre can offer a genuinely

moving and exciting experience. But not for the audience. 'Soundscapes by DJ Barney'? Sweet Jesus. I bet you my kidneys that the Classical is a bit of swirly strings when Sally prances around, and the 'edgy' urban music (i.e. something by Roni Size from about 1997) is played by Barney during the interval to drown out the sound of the audience walking out. I have been to The New Place (founded 1977) before, and intimate is the word. You have to duck and sprint across the back of the stage if you need a pee during the show. I imagine 'sumptuous' means they've hung up a bit of velvet curtain and will keep the lights low. Don't suppose I can lure you to this? The only thing more horrifying than the thought of the show is the thought of the audience. If anyone deserves to suffer through this, it's people who like and admire David Fauntleroy. I don't mean to sound smug and snotty about this, but I am, so I do.

Aghast

Martin

P.S. Loud spinning noises coming from direction of the cemetery. Wonder what that is? And I don't even like Tennyson ...

P.P.S. I am still hoping the reference to Barney as 'underground' is an attempt at humour. His dad, for God's sake, owns a very expensive boat club in Henley. They live in a glass-fronted barn with a tennis court.

On Monday at 15:23 Martin wrote:

No reply? We better move fast if you want tickets.

On Monday at 16:04 Lucy wrote:

Hi, Martin,
Sorry? I think I missed an email somewhere. Hope it was nothing important.
Lots of love,
Lucy

On Monday at 16:05 Martin wrote:

Oh shit! You won't believe what I think I've done…

On Tuesday at 11:13 Sally wrote:

Dear Martin,
Thanks for your emails. Nice to get your real opinion for once. I think you will be pleasantly surprised by the play. There is, of course, no pressure to come. In fact, if this is your real attitude, don't bother. Why do you have to be so negative about everything?
Sally

Mortified

On Tuesday at 11:15 Martin wrote:

Sally
I am so sorry. What can I say? I was having fun with the flyer, not the play. I'm really looking forward to it. Genuinely. I couldn't feel worse.
Martin

P.S. I'm not negative about everything. I just feel very positive about expressing my negative feelings.

On Wednesday at 11:56 Sally replied:

Martin,
I prefer it when you're at least being honest. Even if your attempts at humour do reveal a nervous, rather insecure little man. It's easy to criticise when you're a sarcastic observer. How is the book coming, by the way? Or do you only write snotty emails nowadays?
　　Sally x

Still Mortified

On Thursday at 9:11 Martin wrote:

I'm still really sorry.

On Thursday at 12:15 Martin wrote:

Sally
Writing to apologise again. I am embarrassed and ashamed
of myself. I'm really looking forward to the play, and I'm sure
you in particular will be excellent. There is nothing funny about
David's surname. Tennyson needed updating. Barney is very
underground.
Sorry
Martin

P.S. I don't suppose we're all still on for the picnic on Sunday?
I promise to bring loads of stuff. And it will be a chance to meet
the new housemate...

On Friday at 11:22 Sally wrote:

Take it back about the hair, and you can come.

On Friday at 11:27 Martin wrote:

Glad you're being big about this. By the way, it's a free
country, and you can't stop me going to the park.

44

On Friday at 11:32 Sally wrote:

Not time for you to stop grovelling yet. David's hair is ...

On Friday at 13:46 Martin wrote:

David's hair is nice and fuzzy and keeps his head warm.
It also adds a welcome three inches to his height. I like it. In
no way does he resemble nightmarish children's entertainer
Pennywise the Clown. I said NO WAY.
See you Sunday.
Martin

P.S. Fauntleroy???

On Friday at 15:34 Sally wrote:

Good enough. I wish you hadn't said that about Pennywise
shudders. See you Sunday. Will call to confirm. I will expect
an excellent array of sandwiches and refreshments from you,
Sargent.

Sally

On Friday at 16:02 Martin wrote:

Great, I'm looking forward to seeing David again too. I have
a project to discus with him. Fancy being in my Garage/Two-
Step version of *The Pickwick Papers*? Mr Pickwick's brother has
been killed by paedophile drugs dealers (led by the sinister Mr
Winkle), and he gets together a gang of vigilantes ('The Pickwick
Club') to mete out bloody yet picaresque revenge...

45

On Friday at 16:03 Sally wrote:

Don't push it, Martin Sargent.

Ross

On Friday at 16:16 Lucy wrote:

Hey, Brother,

Hope you got things sorted out with Sally. Again. Your subconscious seems to be doing a very good job of sabotaging your attempts to get back together. I'm not sure whether I'll be able to make it to the play, sorry about that.

How's the new flatmate?

Lots of love,

Lucy

On Saturday at 11:24 Martin replied:

Hi Luce

Things going well with Ross thus far. He moved his stuff in yesterday and hasn't manifested any obvious signs of freakishness. I was a little perturbed when he brought out a samurai sword and wanted to hang it over the TV, but at least we now have a TV to hang it over. He cooks too! We established fairly swiftly that Philip Hayward is a mutual acquaintance, rather than an actual mate. Ross was at uni with him, but claims to have been trying to shake him since more or less the second half of Freshers' Week 1997. I did wonder if Ross would be able to shed any light on the mystery of what Philip is or does that makes him think he's so terribly special. Unfortunately, he is as puzzled about that as I am. As far as either of us can tell the chief ingredients of Philip's personality seem to be a very loud voice and a total immunity from self-doubt. Worryingly, though, Ross does approve of his taste in jumpers

It would be great if you could come to the play. I'm sure Sally would love to see you. Perhaps you could have a quiet word with her about David.

Love

Martin

On Saturday at 11:26 Lucy replied:

Raining here, so checking my timetable online and waiting for CD:UK to come on. I'll see about the play. Samurai sword?

On Saturday at 12:01 Martin replied:

Ross is still asleep, and I decided to help him unpack by putting his books on the shelf in the living room. I think I have made a terrible discovery. The clues: Haruki Murakami, Yukio Mishima, Milan Kundera, Hunter S. Thompson, biography of Serge Gainsbourg. Opinion?

On Saturday at 12:33 Lucy replied:

Sorry, couldn't respond until I'd seen the backstage report from the Westlife show at Wembley and caught up with U2 on tour in Japan. Charts rotten. Another hour wasted.

Don't get it. What's wrong with Ross's books? *nervously checking bookshelves*

On Saturday at 12:35 Martin replied:

Well, ONE interpretation is that late-sleeping Ross is a broad-minded hipster with varied literary tastes and an interest in hard-living French crooners.

On Saturday at 12:37 Lucy wrote:

Is that not a good thing? What is the other possibility?

On Saturday at 12:39 Martin wrote:

The other possibility is that he buys all his books in HMV.

On Saturday at 12:40 Lucy wrote:

Horrors!

Mortified Again

On Monday at 9:10 Martin wrote:

Sally
I'm so sorry. What can I say, except that it was a genuine
accident. Ross is completely embarrassed, and so am I. Other
than that one incident, I thought the picnic was lovely. I hope
the wait at A and E wasn't too long, and that David is feeling
OK.
Sorry, sorry, sorry
Martin

On Monday at 10:05 Sally replied:

I'm not very impressed with you, but it wasn't entirely your
fault, so there's no need to over-apologise. David's not feeling
too great, actually. He has two black eyes and a broken nose, and
he's being interviewed about the play today.
Sally

On Monday at 10:10 Martin wrote:

Hi David
Writing to say I hope you are feeling a little better today,
and good luck with the interview. It was good to see you
and Sally yesterday, and I really enjoyed the day, apart from
the unfortunate incident. I can't apologise enough for what
happened, and I can only assure you that it was a genuine
accident, and that Ross was only trying to help. It was a very

stupid idea of me to bring the football.

Really looking forward to seeing the play.
Get well soon.
Martin

On Monday at 10:18 Martin wrote:

Hi Ross

Sally's email is s_kendle@demon.com, if you have a moment
to email today. David can be contacted via his website or
frequentflyer@hotmail.com. Apparently his nose is broken and
he has two black eyes. I've already dropped them a line, and I
think they would appreciate it if you did too.

By the way, there wasn't any milk this morning. If you're
around the flat today, it would be great if you could pick some
more up.
Cheers
Martin

Clash of Personalities

On Monday at 11:31 Lucy wrote:

So how was the picnic? Did you dazzle and outshine Dreadful David? Was Ross a hit?

On Monday at 13:45 Martin replied:

Ross was a hit all right. We managed to send David to casualty with a broken nose and two black eyes.

On Monday at 14:14 Lucy replied:

What, intentionally?

On Monday at 14:16 Martin replied:

Unfortunately not.

It was all going fine: lovely day, excellent spread from M&S, decent bottle of sparkling wine. Ross was telling us about his last flatmate, who he reckons was an undiagnosed obsessive-compulsive. Ross is a pretty funny bloke, full of plans and ideas. I got a few good lines in, too. Even David wasn't being too dastardly, although he did insist on hand-feeding Sally grapes. Then I decided to tempt the gods by getting the football out and suggesting a kick-around. The rest, in true sitcom style, is perfectly predictable. We were all a bit drunk and lively, and some of us (I admit) may have been feeling a bit over-competitive.

To cut a long story short: we were one-nil down, the ball was in the air, David, Ross and I all went for it. I managed to slam into David from behind, and then Ross, going for the header, managed to connect forehead to nose with David. He went down. Recriminations were thrown.

Which was when Ross did the unthinkable. David was having a sit-down, with Sally fussing around with towels and ice. He reckoned his nose was broken, so we all had a look at it, and it was definitely a bit swollen. Ross, having taken a look at it, asks whether David had heard a crack when they collided. David thought that he had. With no further ado Ross reaches over and twists David's nose, hard, to the right. There is definitely a crack this time.

David, understandably, gets in a right old sulk. Exit David and Sally to casualty, David threatening to sue us for assault. Ross and I did offer to come with them and explain what had happened, but we were informed our presence would be surplus to requirements.

So David gets nursed and fussed over by Sally, while I get accused of having encouraged Ross to assault him. A disappointing result.

Hope things going better with you.

Lots of Love

Martin

Do the Crunch

On Wednesday at 14:45 Barney wrote:

Hi Mart,
I heard about Sunday's antics. Guess you aren't over Sally yet, eh? I've composed a little track in honour of the occasion (see attached file). I think (humbly) it's pretty good. It's a kind of punk-dance thing. Dunce, if you will. Let me know what you think.
Regards, Pards,
Barney

On Thursday at 11:16 Martin replied:

Cheers for this, Barney. Very sensitive of you. Have you sent it to David?
I thought it was quite funny, but I'm not sure it's actually legal to have a record which instructs its readers to 'take your partner by the hand', 'hold them close' and 'headbutt them on the nose'. There may also be health and safety objections to having everyone 'form a circle, turn around, punch a stranger to the ground'. I would very much like to be there if you play it at your next night. I should add, of course, that I would be sitting that particularly tune out at the bar.
Martin

The *Chalk Farm Gazette*

On Wednesday at 12:45 Martin wrote:

Hi Sally

I've just seen the *Chalk Farm Gazette*. Nice interview with David, very probing and not at all adulatory. Who wrote it? His auntie?

I was a bit surprised to learn from the article that you and David are officially an item now. Is this a serious thing or a publicity stunt?

Good photo of David. I think the black eyes suit him. I hope he's recovering, anyway.

Regards

Martin

On Wednesday at 13:34 Sally replied:

Hello, Martin,

No, the article wasn't written by his auntie. Yes, David and I are 'officially' an item now, and no, it isn't a publicity stunt.

Lots of people have been in touch to say they've seen the article, and to enquire about poor David's eyes. He's doing well - the swelling's going down, and has gone from red and black to iridescent green and bright yellow, which is apparently normal. I shall be quite glad when he has recovered - he's being a bit 'dramatic' about the whole thing. Apparently a few friends weren't taken in by the version of events in the article, and have been in touch with David to see if I've been beating him. Please thank Ross again for the flowers and chocolates.

Love,

Sally

On Wednesday at 13:42 Martin wrote:

Hi Ross

Hope you're having a productive day. I sent David and Sally the flowers/chocolate as we discussed. If you want to split it, it came to about a fiver each.

By the way, sorry to be boring, but I think the gas bill is a bit overdue. I put a cheque in the envelope on the kitchen table. It would be great if we could get that sent off today.

Cheers

Martin

On Wednesday at 13:46 Martin wrote:

Hi Luce

I'm forwarding you the latest email from Sally. Please note that she has started signing off with 'love' again. That probably means there is still hope, right?

Martin

On Thursday at 14:23 Lucy wrote:

Thanks for sending me the latest from Sally. Yes, Martin, that is a very exciting development. I would draw your attention to the rest of the email, however, i.e. the bit about her having a new boyfriend.

Tell me more about the article, though.

Love,

Lucy

On Thursday at 19:14 Martin replied:

Hey Luce

You're right. I think in retrospect that I got a bit over-excited

about Sally's sign-off. I'm writing from the flat. I'm not sure
where Ross is. He was supposed to be writing at home today
- apparently there's a producer interested in his idea for a sitcom
about the romantic entanglements of a group of G8 protestors
- but there's no sign of him. Gas bill not paid - grrr. Also no
milk again. Perhaps he got kidnapped as he was about to clean
all his stuff out of the living room. Or perhaps he decided to
have a go at cleaning the loo, and it got him before he got it. The
bathroom's a bit of a shocker too at the moment - I found a three-
inch-high mushroom growing under the sink yesterday, and I'm
not sure whether to clean the bath or shave it (yuck, sorry).

I'll save the article about David for you, but here are some
edited 'highlights', courtesy of Rachel Farnaby of the *Chalk Farm
Gazette*:

*

I'm surprised when David Fauntleroy, whose radical reworking
of Tennyson's 'The Lady of Shalott' starts next week at the New
Place, enters the café where our interview is to take place. I'm
not surprised by the fact he is talking excitedly on his mobile -
after all, he is a busy man these days, with the final rehearsals
under way for the play (and as I discover he has plenty more
ideas buzzing around his fertile brain for future projects). Nor
by the way he greets me - a howl of recognition that turns
heads, followed by a kiss on both cheeks. Nor am I surprised
(although I was a little disappointed) that he is accompanied
by a gorgeous creature called Sally - his current leading lady
- who obviously dotes on him. Nor am I surprised at his outfit:
standard director's uniform, although with a personal twist:
long college-style scarf, corduroy combats, and a military-
style jumper, set off with a heavy belt with a crescent-moon-
shaped silver buckle. I am surprised to see one of London's
most talked-about young directors sporting a magnificent pair
of black eyes.

I ask where he got the shiners. He is properly modest, but
it turns out he was forced to defend someone's honour. Sally,
who is an elegant blonde, blushes. He doesn't want to talk
about it, he says: 'It's nothing Dr Theatre can't take care of.'

When I ask whether it's a case of 'You should have seen the other guy' he merely gives me a charming smile. 'Guys, plural,' he admits, before asking if he can get me anything to eat. 'The strawberry shortcake here is a little miracle,' he tells me, changing the subject.

He's modest about his background. 'It's all very boring,' he says. 'Like most people I did English at Cambridge.'

I ask Sally whether she worried what people would think about her stepping out with the director. After all, it's on page one of the book of theatrical clichés.

David jumps in. 'I don't think anyone who knows Sally and I would question the sincerity and solidity of our relationship,' he says. He pauses, thoughtfully, and squeezes her hand. 'I know it sounds corny, but we really are soul-mates.'

There's something in the way he says it that reinvigorates the old-fashioned sentiment. Yours truly admits to feeling, at that moment, a little stab of jealousy.

I end by asking what's next for Sally and David.

'Professionally?' he asks 'Or personally?'

His meteoric rise is not likely to stop any time soon. He's already working on a TV project (with a big-name actor I've been sworn to keep a secret, because they haven't yet committed), and has a play he is hoping to unveil at next year's Edinburgh Festival.

'It's really very early stages,' he explains 'But I can reveal it's a little bit political, and deals with contemporary issues of race, gender, religion and sexuality.'

And will Sally be starring in it?

'You'll have to ask her,' he says, with a twinkle in his eye. 'I certainly hope so.'

It's impossible, meeting this charming couple, to wish them anything but the greatest of success together.

As we are leaving, ever the gentleman, David helps me into my coat. I notice he smells delicious, a little like freshly baked bread. 'I was making some scones for Sally this morning,' he reveals, when I comment.

'Don't make too much of the eye thing,' he smiles. 'It's not what I want people to focus on. It's really the play that matters, not anything personal about me. It's my work that I want to be remembered by. I hate all this culture of celebrity nowadays. All I want is for people to enjoy my plays, and, if it doesn't sound too arrogant, to change people's lives. After all, I think that's what theatre, real theatre, is there for.'

From anyone else this might indeed sound a little arrogant. But in the case of David Fauntleroy, I think he's being much too modest.

***

The photo's a stinker, too: they've got David posing like a boxer in front of a poster for his play, with his shiners on display. He looks like a pugnacious panda, or perhaps like something the NSPCC should know about.

I can confirm that it is certainly not 'impossible' to wish this charming couple anything but the greatest success.

Lots of Love

Martin

Solidarity

On Friday at 11:30 Martin wrote:

Dear Ella/Mike/Chris (and Emily)

Apologies for the group email. Writing to let you know about Sally's play next week (see attached flyer). I know Thursday nights are a pain, but I'm sure she'd really appreciate a show of support. I'm going to be there, and it would be great to have some backup. Apparently the cast and crew are going on for karaoke after, and we are also invited. Hope you are all well.

Best

Martin

On Friday at 11:35 Martin wrote:

Hey Laura

End of the week at last! Sending you the attached on the off-chance you are free next week. Getting a bunch of people together to go, so let me know if you fancy it.

Martin

On Friday at 11:41 Ella wrote:

Hey, Martin

Thanks for the invite. I'm afraid I can't make it. I'm writing an article for G2 about what it's like to avoid all cultural stimulation for a week. Would be great to see you soon, though, and give my best to Sally.

Lots of love, Ella

On Friday at 12:05 Martin replied:

Really? Good luck with the article. How long have you been planning this little experiment?

On Friday at 12:11 Ella replied:

I just came up with the idea, actually. See you soon. Hope you're taking good care of yourself.

On Friday at 12:34 Mike wrote:

Hi, Martin,
Thanks for the invitation. Play sounds great, but not sure what I'm doing. I often have work things on Thursday, but I'll let you know next week.
Best,
Mike

On Friday at 13:06 Chris replied:

Hey, Martin,
Thanks for the invite. I don't want to come, because the play sounds rubbish. Not being funny, but you've broken up with Sally, which means you no longer have to do things like this. I'd love to come and be supportive, but I'm not willing to pay £7.50. Sorry not to think up an excuse. No doubt Emily will be bothered to think one up - can we assume it counts for me (too)? By the way, she's going to be a bit upset about being put in brackets.

Mate, over the last year you have invited us to come and see: a punk band covering Bulgarian folksongs; two poetry readings; a showcase for new ventriloquists at something called the Giggle Club; and an exhibition on the meaning of Frenchness despite

the fact we're not French. Can we not simply go for a pint
sometime?

Saw the *Chalk Farm Gazette*, and very sorry to hear about
Sally.

Chris

On Friday at 13:42 Martin replied:

Cheers for your honesty, mate. How about a pint next week,
then? There's an old coaching inn in the East End that has
a Dickens theme and serves Victorian drinks. How about an
evening getting uncommon lushey on shrub or half-and-half?

On Friday at 15:07 Chris replied:

Yes, that would be an option. Alternatively there's a
contemporary-themed pub on the high street near me that serves
contemporary-themed drinks. Why not experiment with that?

On Friday at 15:11 Emily wrote:

Hi Martin

Chris and I were saying only last night how much we'd love to
see you. I'm afraid I think we have a dinner party (snore snore)
that evening, otherwise it would be lovely. Send my love to Sally.

Hope you are well, and thinking of you,

Emily

(PS. Why am I in brackets?)

On Friday at 15:14 Martin replied:

Dear (Emily)

Sorry about the brackets. Actually I've already heard back from Chris. He didn't mention the dinner party, but we said we'd meet for a pint soon. Just a pint, no New Iranian Cinema or Czech Animation. I'll give your best to Sally, and try to think up a decent excuse why you're not there. You guys should co-ordinate your excuses better.

Lots of Love

Martin

On Friday at 15:23 Emily replied:

Oops. Well, I guess that makes us even for the brackets thing. See you soon,

Emily

On Friday at 16:45 Laura wrote:

The play sounds like it should be interesting. Count me in. Have a good weekend, and looking forward to next week.

Lots of love,

Laura

Lack of Solidarity

On Monday at 10:03 Martin wrote:

Hi Lucy

Any chance at all you can make it on Thursday? I'm willing to reimburse your train fare etc. Only £5 on door for students. I'd really appreciate it. I was trying to get a gang of people together but everyone's ducking out, with the exception of Laura.
Hope all going well.
Martin

On Monday at 11:34 Lucy replied:

Hi, Martin,

Really don't think I can make it. Miriam's having a dinner party and I already said I'd go. Why not just go with the lovely Laura?

Sorry to be crap,
Lucy

On Monday at 14:02 Martin replied:

Hi Lucy

I don't suppose the dinner party is a scheme you've devised to entrap this Sam guy you mentioned on the phone?

I had lunch with Laura today, and despite my attempts to suggest an alternate plan, she is definitely up for coming. The problem, as I see it, is now twofold:

1) I promised mates, and have come up with none. Thus to

Laura I am going to look like a right Billy.

2) This also lends a creepy vibe to the fact I am going to Sally's play with her, and makes it look like I am doing it because Sally is going out with Bilbo the ginger theatre hobbit.

But if I don't go, it will look like I am a) upset about the article and about Sally moving on and b) not interested in Laura.

Suggestions?

Love

Martin

On Monday at 14:04 Lucy replied:

Why not take Mum?

On Monday at 14:14 Martin replied:

Great. Thanks a lot for that brilliant suggestion. Good luck with Sam on Thursday. After all I've done for you...

On Monday at 14:59 Lucy replied:

Not my fault you got no mates. Perhaps if you stopped insisting people come to evenings of satirical puppetry and Belgian chanson ...

Only joking, and sorry not to be able to make it. As you guessed, the dinner party is a fiendish scheme to ensnare the lovely Sam from down the corridor. He doesn't stand a chance against my seafood risotto and little black dress.

Let me know how it goes on Thursday, and good luck,

Lucy

PS: Not quite sure what you meant by 'all you have done for me'. To which of the following incidents are you referring?

1. When I was four and you told me Mum and Dad got me at

the Spastics shop?

2. When I was six and you told me you'd overheard them saying they wanted to take me back 'cos I was defective, but they'd lost the receipt?

3. The numerous times you asked me to play hide-and-seek with you and your friends, only after about an hour I realised no one was looking for me?

4. The time when I was eight and you told Mum and Dad I was sleeping in the back seat of the car, and they left me for two hours at a French service-station?

5. The time when Michael came to take me to see *American Pie* and you told him I was 'upstairs having a shave'?

6. Or perhaps the time I stayed with you at college and you did the 'Bombardiez gag' on me? That joke is so lame, by the way.

On Monday at 15:02 Martin replied:

Bitter?

On Monday at 15:14 Martin wrote:

Hi Ross
Sending you the flyer for Sally's play. I'm sure you'd be very welcome.
Martin

P.S. By the way, I hope you're not dead. Didn't see you all weekend and there's a bit of an odd smell in the flat. If you are, no need to come on Thursday.

On Monday at 15:58 Martin wrote:

Hi Martin-in-IT

It's the other Martin here. Don't suppose you are interested in coming to a play on Thursday? Ask other people too, if you'd like.

Martin Sargent

\------------------------

On Tuesday at 9:05 Martin wrote:

Hey Luce

Bollocks. I think in desperation I may have made a major tactical error. I suspect what you always say is right, and at some subconscious level I wish myself serious ill. Possibly guilt over my childhood treatment of you? I know it means nothing to you, but if you talk to Mum please ask her to send up a quick prayer for Martin Sergeant to be busy on Thursday.

On the other hand, I should add that I hold you personally responsible for this predicament. I regret ever having told Mum and Dad you weren't in the back seat. You should thank me - if I hadn't mentioned it you'd now be living off discarded croques messieurs and flat Orangina and sleeping in a unisex public toilet outside Calais.

Cheers
Martin

\------------------------

What the Hell is a Goth Barbecue?

On Wednesday at 10:58 Lucy wrote:

It must be Karma. Without consulting me Miriam has decided to make the dinner party fancy dress. Not only that, the theme is Goth. Brilliant. Now not only will I be dressed as Morticia Adams but Sam will be wearing eyeliner and white makeup. Drat. Well, it may be worth it to see what Miriam's boyfriend wears. I bet you it's either drag or his old lab coat. Any suggestions for a sexy Goth costume? (Imagine I am not your sister.) Don't say big white sheet.

\-

On Wednesday at 11:14 Martin wrote:

Why not be a sexy cat? Everyone loves a sexy cat.

\-

On Wednesday at 12:05 Lucy wrote:

Thanks. Of course I'd already thought of that, but Miriam has explicitly vetoed sexy cats, horny devils and mad scientists. Is there such a thing as a sexy zombie? I got a worrying text from Sam a minute ago asking if I have any black nail varnish.

\-

On Wednesday at 12:32 Lucy wrote:

Better and better. Now it's not a dinner party in my kitchen, it's a barbecue in Christine's garden. A Goth barbecue. Surely that's a contradiction in terms? AND the weather forecast is rain. I bet the whole fiasco is Miriam trying to get in with Christine and the pink-shirt gang on the third floor. I can't sum up Christine better than by reporting that she spent the first term trying to get everyone to call her 'Minxy' and claiming it was her family nickname. I bet you anything it's not.

Then she claimed everyone on her corridor was ignoring her and got her parents to buy her a flat. Her unpopularity may have been to do with a series of her horse-faced one-night-stands puking in the kitchen and showers and the fact that she reported us all to the warden for using her Maldon Sea Salt. She's not even properly posh! She can't get her collar to stay turned up and has a weird ruddy face like bacon. I don't like her very much. I've texted Miriam suggesting we make it a crap Sloane party, but haven't got a reply yet.

By the way, who is Martin Sergeant? Have you developed an alter-ego? If you're creating a secret identity to fight crime may I suggest that you go a bit further than merely changing the spelling of our surname?

Just a thought,

Lucy

Thursday Night

On Wednesday at 12:40 Mike wrote:

Alright, Chum,
Sorry to say that it turns out I'd forgotten I have a do
with work people tomorrow night. Sorry about that. Let's do
something soon. Not this weekend, I have paintballing with the
gang from the office. By the way, how's your sister?
Mike

On Wednesday at 12:45 Martin wrote:

Mike, you had 24 hours to come up with an excuse and that's
all you could think of? Also: paintballing? You are so corporate.
'Oh no, you got me again, boss. Wow, you're really good at this.
Ooh, I missed. Ooh, I missed again.' I hope you get thoroughly
splattered. Stay away from my sister, you slimy suit. How's your
mum?
Martin

On Wednesday at 12:47 Mike wrote:

My mum has cancer, and I really do have a work thing
tomorrow.

On Wednesday at 13:03 Martin wrote:

Mate, I am so sorry, I hadn't heard. Please give your mum my best and let her know I'm thinking of her. It must be incredibly tough - if you want to meet up for a chat, give me a bell. Really sorry about that. I'm wigging a bit about tomorrow night, if that's any excuse. Long story.

Best Wishes

Martin

On Wednesday at 13:05 Mike wrote:

Ha ha.

Wow, you are such a sensitive guy. You deal with serious issues really well, you know that? My mum is fine, but I'll let her know you're 'thinking of her'. Be careful when and where you do so, freakzone.

'Best Wishes' is such a dipstick way to sign off, by the way.

Mike

PS 'corporate'? 'you slimy suit'? Kurt's dead, man, Kurt's dead.

On Wednesday at 16:29 Martin Sergeant wrote:

Hi, Other Martin,

Thank you for the invite. I'm not going to be able to make it. I've got back together with my ex, so I'm moving my stuff back in. Which isn't a euphemism.

Best wishes,

Martin

Part Three
Special Friends

The Fear

The Ballad of Martin Sargent

The 'Bombardiez' Gag Explained

The Play

Aftermath

On Friday at 7:15 Elizabeth Sargent wrote:

Hello, Martin,

How was the play? I heard you took a 'special friend'. Ooh, very exciting. Can't wait to hear all about it. And have you heard anything about Lucy's barbecue? Dad sends his love.

Love,

Mum

PS: I did the prayers last Sunday and slipped in one for Lady. She doesn't seem to be suffering much, but is getting very slow and sleepy. Taking her to the vet tomorrow. I said one for you as well – I hope you don't mind.

On Friday at 9:42 Martin replied:

Hi Mum

Sorry again to hear about Lady, and thanks for thinking of me too. Had a good time last night - we ended up going on to karaoke after the show. Play wasn't much cop, but a good time was had by all. Haven't heard about Lucy's barbecue yet - it being 9:42 in the morning. Speak at weekend.

Love

Martin

P.S. I wish you wouldn't use the phrase 'special friend' - her name is Laura, and she isn't retarded.

On Friday at 9:44 Martin wrote:

Hi Lucy

Hope the Goth barbecue went well. I had an email from Mum asking about last night. Just got into work, and still a bit shaky. Very hazy recollections of last night, although it definitely involved karaoke later on. There was a taxi, too. Woke up with Leonard Cohen on my ipod, which is never a good sign, but as far as I can recall I behaved myself. Don't think there was a snog. Lots of Love

Martin

P.S. Apparently Mum mentioned me in her prayers on Sunday. God knows what she said. Ha ha, I reread that. Still a bit drunk, to tell the truth.

On Friday at 9:46 Martin wrote:

Hi Laura

Hope you had a good time last night (and aren't suffering as much as I am this morning). Fancy meeting later for (light) lunch and to try to piece together what actually happened?

Martin

On Friday at 9:52 Martin wrote:

Hi Ross

Hope I didn't wake you up banging around this morning. I'm a bit of a state still. Thanks for coming - I hope it wasn't too awful. I remember us doing karaoke together and there being a bit of kerfuffle with someone about the tambourine we hired. Let me know if you recall any more.

Martin

On Friday at 9:55 Martin wrote:

Hi Sally

I wanted to say (although I'm sure I said so last night) how much I enjoyed the play (and thanks for inviting us to the karaoke). Hope it wasn't weird to bring Laura. Not quite sure about the sequence of events, so would be great if you could help me putting the pieces together. Better go and get on with some work at last.

Lots of Love

Martin

P.S. Have just remembered that you helped put me in the taxi, I think. Cheers. Not quite sure how I ended up getting so wasted. I seem to recall some shots of tequila - hope you feel less dreadful than me! Congratulations again on the show.

P.P.S. Do I owe you money for the karaoke?

On Friday at 10:02 Martin wrote:

All right Barney

Well done for last night. What happened? Starting to sober up, and feeling the fear coming on.

Martin

The Dark Side

On Friday at 11:32 Ross wrote:

hy mutton, bswv ciou chuihnwoic cxniowuec. cuiwnwicu.
yghyubuin. ucnhuiwhcuiw cuionwoc ichnuiwe coihjweo.
fhyfhiw. yhtrnendi. biewhbic. ncuiewncwei. ugh. urrrgh. aaargh.
feel shit. yours truly, ross. p.s. i woke up with the tambourine.
who paid for the taxi?

On Friday at 12:06 Barney wrote:

Alright Chief,
Bloody hell, wouldn't want to be you this morning, wild
man. Not sure those tequilas agreed with you. I think you went
to the dark side a little bit. Bloody good night, though. Do you
remember the karaoke? I have to say you were the evening's star
turn. Not sure your bird was too impressed, though.
Rock on, Obi Wan,
Barney

PS cheers for the suggestions for a DJ name. Hope you don't
mind me using them.

On Friday at 12:13 Martin replied:

Barney
Seriously, is this a wind-up? Did I piss Sally off? Is it
something to do with the tambourine?
Martin

On Friday at 12:17 Barney replied:

No wind-up, but don't worry about it. You were a bit lively, that's all. What I want to know is what you said to David at the urinal. It was after you accused him of hogging the tambourine and tried to pour beer on him, and before you fell off the table. He looked pretty weirded out, and Laura didn't look too impressed. Sally was, I would say, more resigned about the whole thing. By the way, I didn't know you speak Japanese.

On Friday at 12:20 Martin replied:

Urinal? Bloody hell, I'd like to know too. Did he say anything about it to you? Also: Why was I on the table in order to fall off it?

I don't speak Japanese.

On Friday at 12:30 Barney replied:

Well, you were on the table to demonstrate your Jagger dance. You'd just got everyone's attention when you went over and took all the drinks with you. That was when you managed to whack Laura in the contact lens. So we were all looking for it and I thought you were too, but it turned out that you were looking for the slice of lemon peel you 'slipped' on, in order to prove you weren't drunk.

You were certainly claiming to be able to speak Japanese last night. You went off to find the management at one point in order to tell them we wanted another hour, and claimed you would negotiate a discount with your mastery of the language. Bit odd since the people at the desk weren't actually Japanese.

We went to look for you after about forty minutes and you were doing 'Ghostbusters' in someone else's booth. They looked pretty unimpressed, even when you explained that your dad knew Ray Parker Jr.

That, I think, was when the management asked you to leave.

No idea what role the tambourine played in the evening's events.

Does your dad really know Ray Parker Jr?

On Friday at 12:32 Martin replied:

Of course my dad doesn't know Ray Parker Jr. Things are coming back to me now. Let me know if you remember anything else - I'm going to the loo for a cry and then I'm going to find Laura and apologise.

On Friday at 13:34 Martin wrote:

Ross

Memories from last night keep lurching out of the brain-fog like zombie pirates, and they ain't pretty. No sign of Laura at work today. I need you to tell me all you remember. In particular: Do you know what I said to David at the urinal? Did Laura find her contact? Was she pissed off? What is the full story of the tambourine? Were we thrown out because of me? Do you think it was me who paid for the taxi?

Martin

On Friday at 13:45 Martin wrote:

Dear Laura

I am so sorry about last night. The evening didn't quite turn out as anticipated. I hope you are feeling OK. I feel extremely bad, in all senses of the word.

Yours Sincerely

Martin

On Friday at 13:48 Martin wrote:

Oh shit. The girl who sits opposite Laura just walked past and gave me an absolutely filthy look. Filthy in the sense of 'you twat', I mean. Ross, I think I have done bad and foolish things.

On Friday at 14:30 Ross replied:

Still drunk, and have a tingle all down one arm. In answer to your previous questions: Yes, I do know what you said to David at the urinal. You explained it to me and the taxi driver on the way home. Sally gave you twenty quid to pay for the taxi, I think, and you gave the driver a fiver of your own. That was after we were asked to leave, and you tried to hide in someone else's booth. You gave your position away by singing the *Ghostbusters* theme tune, and then declared they couldn't throw you out because you were a family friend of Ray Parker Jr. Surprisingly, that didn't work.

Laura didn't find her contact lens, and declined your invitation for a nightcap. I think Sally and David gave her a lift home. I'm not an expert on feminine psychology, but I believe that she was indeed rather pissed off.

The tale of the tambourine is as follows. You wanted us all to hire them, but there turned out to be a four quid deposit, so only you got one, but promised to share it around. Then you had a row with David because you accused him of hogging it, and you poured beer on him. I believe David had taken the tambourine into safe-keeping because you'd been hitting him on the head with it. After we were thrown out you declared moral victory because you had hidden the tambourine under your shirt. Then you did a little dance on the pavement and made up a song about it, which you sang at the bouncer. Which was when Sally put you in the taxi. So in effect you bought a tambourine for four quid. When we got home you conferred it on me, quite tearfully, as a solemn symbol of our mateship.

Hope this helps.

On Friday at 14:40 Martin replied:

Oh God! But how come Sally and David were driving?

On Friday at 14:43 Ross replied:

Because they weren't drinking all night. Which is why you had their tequilas. I forgot to tell you your account of what you said to David at the urinal. You rushed out and followed him when he went to the loo. Then, apparently, you stood next to him and said 'Massive cock.' He replied 'Thanks', and you said 'No, I don't mean you *have* a massive cock, I mean you *are* a massive cock.' Class. The taxi driver thought it was hilarious, which I think was why you over-tipped him.

On Friday at 14:47 Martin replied:

Bloody hell. Although I shudder to ask, do you remember me making suggestions of a DJ name for Barney? When was that?

On Friday at 14:49 Ross replied:

I certainly do. It was when we were walking from the pub to the karaoke and you were beginning to go to the bad. He wanted to know whether we preferred DJ Asbo or DJ Anarchitect. Laura came up with DJ Dinner Jacket, and I had DJ Mike Hunt. You suggested DJ Taylor, then declared you had a 'genius one', but were laughing too much to tell us. You prefaced it by saying it was a reference to Dostoyevsky and Iggy Pop.

On Friday at 14:51 Martin replied:

Don't muck about. What was it?

On Friday at 14:54 Ross replied:

DJ Idiot. He seemed pretty taken with the idea, actually.

On Friday at 14:55 Martin replied:

Please tell me I didn't do the 'Bombardiez' gag on anyone.

On Friday at 14:57 Ross replied:

That depends what the 'Bombardiez' gag is.

On Friday at 15:00 Martin replied:

Don't worry. You'd remember if I'd done it.

On Friday at 15:06 Martin wrote:

Dear Sally

I am so sorry. Again. From what I've pieced together I made a complete idiot of myself. I can only hope I didn't entirely spoil your night. Please pass on my apologies to David for what I said in the urinal. And for knocking all the drinks over. And for getting us thrown out. I owe you twenty quid. I couldn't possibly feel any worse. Thank you so much for taking Laura home. I doubt she was very impressed. Did she say anything to you? Congratulations on the play, as well. It was a very pleasant surprise.

Wretchedly

Martin

On Friday at 15:04 Sally replied:

I can only suppose you're under the impression that you did the 'massive cock' joke on David. In fact, you said 'You have a massive cock', waited for a response and didn't get one, and then said 'No, you *have* a massive cock' again and collapsed in hysterics. He wasn't upset, but he was a bit bewildered. I don't think he much appreciated being referred to as 'Garfunkel' all night, though. Or being repeatedly told to sing something by Simply Red. I take it the 'new blonde' thing has totally passed you by?

Laura seems like a very nice girl. I have to say she didn't appear to be blown away with your charm last night. We got her home safe. I think you owe her an apology too. Or here's a better idea - instead of continually having to apologise to people, why don't you try not being a complete prat?

I take it you don't remember what you sang? Don't bother apologising when you remember. It's very tedious being apologised to all the time, and it puts me in the awkward position of having to either forgive you or act like I'm more upset than I am. You made an idiot of yourself, and I don't think, deep down, that you actually are an idiot, or I wouldn't have gone out with you in the first place. But once again you've managed to make everything all about you.

Get in touch when you're prepared to behave like a human being.

Sally

PS - David and I thanked Ross for the flowers etc and he looked completely blank. I did assume it was all your idea, but you could at least have mentioned to Ross that you were sucking up on his behalf.

PPS - At least you didn't do that stupid 'Bombardiez' gag. Which shows what small mercies I'm nowadays grateful for.

On Friday at 15:07 Martin wrote:

Barney/Ross
For the love of God rack your memories. What did I sing?
Something I sang really rubbed Sally up the wrong way.
Martin

On Friday at 15:09 Ross wrote:

Well, you did a duet with Laura to start. Could that have been
it? I think it was 'Close to You'.

On Friday at 15:11 Martin replied:

No, that would merely have been grossly inappropriate given
the circumstances. To piss Sally off I'd have had to have chosen
something truly awful. Think, boys, think.

On Friday at 15:15 Barney replied:

Well, next you discovered they had Leonard Nimoy's 'The
Ballad of Bilbo Baggins', which you insisted on crooning at
David.

On Friday at 15:17 Martin replied:

That's bad, but I must have done something worse than that.
P.S. Surprised they had Leonard Nimoy. Usually people prefer
his acting.

On Friday at 15:19 Barney replied:

I was very impressed you knew the words, actually. Then you did 'Love Will Tear Us Apart' and 'You Were Always on My Mind', which were directed at Sally.

On Friday at 15:21 Martin replied:

That's not good either, but there must be worse.

On Friday at 15:23 Barney replied:

Then you and Ross did 'This Town Ain't Big Enough for the Both of Us', while hitting David with the tambourine. Nice falsetto, by the way.

On Friday at 15:24 Martin replied:

Bad, bad, bad. Was that it?

On Friday at 15:25 Barney replied:

As far as I remember. You managed about half of 'Let's Spend the Night Together' before the table attacked you.

On Friday at 15:27 Ross wrote:

That's all I can remember. Except you did 'Fill Your Heart' by David Bowie at one point.

On Friday at 15:28 Martin replied:

That would be it.

On Friday at 15:30 Barney wrote:

In fact not many people who listen to *Hunky Dory* realise that song is not actually a Bowie original - it's a cover of a song by Biff Rose and Paul Williams.

On Friday at 15:32 Ross wrote:

I knew that.

On Friday at 15:35 Barney wrote:

I have a slightly creepy ukulele-and-falsetto version of it recorded by Tiny Tim if you want me to send it to you – it was the B-side to 'Tiptoe Thru the Tulips' and appears on the 1968 album *God Bless Tiny Tim*. I sometimes throw it into my set at the end of a night, and it's never failed to clear the dancefloor yet.

On Friday at 15:37 Martin replied:

That's great, Barney, although a bit beside the point. That was the song Sally and I listened to over and over when we went to Cyprus, thus a deliberately painful thing for me to sing. That was rather evil and stupid of me. No wonder she's upset.

On Friday at 15:39 Ross wrote:

That song's *rubbish*.

On Friday at 15:42 Martin wrote:

Still, if you could send me the Tiny Tim version I'd love to hear it. Cheers, Barney.

The 'Bombardiez' Gag

On Friday at 15:50 Ross wrote:

OK OK, the suspense is killing me. What is the 'Bombardiez' gag?

On Friday at 15:52 Martin replied:

It only works in a pub that serves Bombadier bitter. You wait till someone is getting a round in, then ask for a pint of 'Bombardiez'. They go up and order it, and all the old men at the bar laugh at them.

On Friday at 15:54 Ross replied:

Because it's really pronounced Bombadier?

On Friday at 15:56 Martin replied:

Yeah. Actually, it's not the greatest joke ever.

On Friday at 15:59 Ross replied:

No shit. But what happens if the person getting the round just looks at you oddly and says 'I think you'll find it's pronounced "Bombadier"'?

On Friday at 16:02 Martin replied:

Yes, that's the flaw in the 'Bombardiez' gag.

On Friday at 16:03 Ross replied:

To be honest, mate, I think there's more than one flaw in the 'Bombardiez' gag.

On Friday at 16:11 Martin wrote:

Hello All
The girl who works opposite Laura has just walked past again, whistling the *Ghostbusters* theme tune.
Yours Sincerely
Mud in the Office

P.S. I don't suppose anyone fancies phoning in a bomb scare?

Success!

Hi, Martin,

Sorry not to get back to you sooner. In fact, I only got home about an hour ago. From which you may draw the conclusion that the Goth barbecue was a success (as far as I was concerned, anyway). Went back to Sam's, and made the (I think in retrospect wise) decision not to go straight to lectures in a black dress with little spiders stuck all over it, and with my hair backcombed and hair-sprayed. God, if I can pull in that get-up ...

Obviously none of Christine's mates made any effort at fancy dress, and it seems she hadn't even told them about it, so it was only me and Miriam dressed like idiots when we first turned up. Felt more casual about this as the night went on. Miriam's boyfriend, Frank, was Frankenstein, and had gone to a lot of effort – perhaps too much effort. It was quite unnerving, in fact. Miriam spent most of the evening wandering around with smears of green all over her. He departed about 4 a.m., still in costume, to get the London train, as he was working this morning.

Sam got the balance pretty right – he was a rather dashing Dracula. Of course, that started a long semi-playful argument with Christine (who was, despite the warning, a sexy cat) about the difference between a Goth party and a Halloween party. It ended with a compromise, with Frank saying he was a Goth dressed up for a Halloween party, and Sam agreeing that he was actually being Dave Vanian out of The Damned. I don't *think* Christine heard me asking loudly whether she had come as a fat cat. Of course we got the usual crowd of randoms (someone had invited a vet, and that was taken as a general declaration we wanted every vet who could be mustered to turn up when the pubs closed. So until they all paired up, passed out or pissed off, you couldn't move without being 'regaled' with gross stories about calving and horseshit told by very drunk and ugly boys wearing lab coats. Twats. But at least it wasn't the dental students). Felt a bit sorry for one of them - he'd obviously and rather sweetly (despite not knowing any of us) given the theme a lot of thought, and was wearing a horned helmet. Then he had to spend the whole evening explaining he wasn't a Viking. He pulled Christine, and the last thing I heard as we left this morning was his voice through the bedroom door explaining about the end of the Roman Empire. I'm not sure whether she knew, but he'd puked profusely in the cloakroom earlier. 'There's bits of chewed-up pasta on my pashmina' was perhaps my favourite quote of the evening.

After Frank(enstein) lumbered off to the train station, Miriam started cracking on to the remaining male at the party, a sinister red-eyed creature called Rupert who may have been asleep. Not impressed with that young lady.

Anyway, on the walk of shame back to Sam's, past smirking milkmen etc etc, he revealed that he's Christine's cousin, so I've been racking my brains all day to see if I said anything indiscreet. Sam offered to walk me back to mine but somehow we ended up getting diverted by the all-night garage and going back to his, despite the fact it's further (he is really sweet, so don't get all faux-protective. Also he could whup your ass). Nice flat, too. But even better the great (if not unexpected) revelation: no one in the family as far as Sam knows has ever called Christine 'Minxy'. In fact (until she went a bit bulimic in the sixth form) her family nickname was 'Chubby Chris'. Brilliant.

So, how was the play? As bad as expected? And more importantly, how did things go with Laura? Was Sally eaten up with envy?

Lots of love,
Lucy

PS: Or do I mean eaten up with jealousy? What is the difference?

Not sure of the difference between envy and jealousy, but I think it's fair to say Sally wasn't exactly eaten up with either.

Laura's not responding to my emails. Either she's playing hard to get or I've managed to fuck things up. I suspect the latter. I managed to knock out one of her contact lenses. Although I think it turned out that it had in fact slid round behind her eyeball. Not sure if that's better or worse.

Going to crawl into bed now and reflect on my sins. Flat an absolute state and no sign of Ross (another participant in last night's fiasco). I was shocked and awed when I saw the hoover in the hall, but I think it simply means that the gasman came and had to get at the meter. Still, at least Ross knows where it is now. Perhaps curiosity will compel him to try to turn it on. I'll leave it there to see. I don't think he has figured out that the little letters with the plastic window and the red writing on have bills inside.

Will call over weekend. Congratulations about the party. I hope you are being sensible etc etc.

Lots of Love

Martin

The Play

Hi, Martin

Had a late breakfast at The Eagle with David and Sally. He really is ghastly, isn't he? He invited me to come round and try his crumpets sometime. Fuck Off! Seriously. It must be quite upsetting that Sally prefers him to you. Heard about your antics on Thursday, and was most amused. It doesn't look like I'm going to be able to avoid this play after all - I'm kicking myself for not having given up culture for a month. Is it as atrocious as I suspect it will be?

    Ella

On Saturday at 14:35 Martin replied:

Hey Ella

Yes, it is pretty upsetting that Sally prefers David to me, although I had hitherto avoided putting it to myself quite so bleakly. I wonder if he's giving her drugged bread? All other options are too painful to contemplate.

As for the play, it depends how low your expectations are. Sally, I have to say, is pretty good. The bits with someone pretending to be a mirror and Sally 'looking into him' were pretty amusing. I only found myself thinking longingly about my own death about three times, which is pretty good for pub theatre. The first time was when someone mentioned the 'round table' and they projected a picture of a set of decks onto the back wall. I'd almost recovered from choking on that particular slice of idiot pie when 'DJ Lance' played 'Ghost Town' by The Specials.

94

Why he did that God only knows, except that all plays with some faint claim to social relevance apparently have to feature it. It's like the third rule of theatre, after 'Make your entrances and exits quick' and 'Never act in anything based on the works of C. S. Lewis or Jerome K. Jerome'. Surely 'Almost Medieval' by the Human League would have been a more logical choice?

Anyway, the sight of the cast faux-skanking around in medieval dress to a song about the plight of the inner cities under Thatcher was fairly unforgettable. Although the man dressed up as a jester who was dancing like Bez may or may not have made a pretty telling point about contemporary culture. That could have been accidental. After that I was sure I could handle anything. Boy, was I wrong. They only went and did 'mime horses'. Although by that time my eyes had rolled back into my head in embarrassment and my toes had retracted into my feet, I think the idea was that Lancelot was riding to save The Lady ('Shally'?). On another actor. She OD'd (or perhaps died of shame) stage right, and he 'galloped' past her on a man in a black polo neck three times. I think that was meant to convey the distance he had to go. Not a dry eye in the house, I tell you. Alas, they didn't play 'Crazy Horses' by the Osmonds. God, it made me realise how much I love television.

Anyway, it's the kind of magic that can only be generated when a paying audience and a team of actors come face to face to waste each other's time in person. I will be laying flowers at the feet on the nearest statue of Oliver Cromwell later on today.

Almost forgot the best bit. Halfway through one of the dance numbers (there were several, but let's not go there. Let's just say that at one point the Lady of Shalott's woe was illustrated by a weeping willow dance to the contemporary club sounds of... Portishead) the door opened and someone in a leather waistcoat wandered onstage from the horrible 90s ciderpunk pub below. Looking a bit bewildered, understandably, he delivered the immortal line 'cigarette machine?' before wandering off again. I don't imagine for a minute I was the only person considering taking advantage of the intrusion to bolt across the stage and escape. Possibly covering my exit by pretending to be a ska-loving medieval peasant who is thoroughly disgruntled with Thatcherite employment policy. That, as David might put it, is the kind of unpredictability and energy you only get with theatre.

But that's only my opinion. You might like it. Anyway, definitely go and show your support. The flyer was certainly right in one respect: I won't ever think about Victorian love poetry in the same way again.
Martin

On Saturday at 14:42 Ella replied:

Thank you for the warning. I guess from the fact you are lurking online on a Saturday afternoon that you haven't heard from this Laura girl since your memorable evening? Pint soon?
Ella

PS It may not be drugged bread. Perhaps David's simply a better lover than you.

On Saturday at 14:45 Martin replied:

Oh THAT was the image I've been frantically repressing for the last few weeks. Cheers, Ella. I disliked David quite enough already without needing to picture him as a nimble-fingered sex wizard.

On Saturday at 14:49 Ella replied:

Let's not go overboard here. I only speculated that he might be better than you.

On Saturday at 14:52 Martin replied:

I'm not even going to ask what Sally's been telling you. Thanks for getting in touch, though. You've really put the finishing boot into my day.

Thursday Night (Again)

Hi Laura

Sorry to bother you again. Writing to apologise again for
my ridiculous and idiotic behaviour on Thursday night. Also, I
probably should also have mentioned that Sally was my ex. Hope
things aren't going to be weird now. I would be very grateful if
we could forget the whole thing ever happened. Anyway, hope
you're having a good weekend.

Martin

On Sunday at 18:23 Laura wrote:

Hi, Martin,

No problem, for goodness sake. Sorry not to get back to you
sooner. An old friend appeared unexpectedly for the weekend, so
I haven't been checking my mail. If you want to forget Thursday
- and I'm surprised you can remember it - that's fine. There are
a few little images it will be hard to erase from the memory,
though - not least your version of 'The Ballad of Bilbo Baggins',
and the spectacular moment you declared 'Oh my God I'm
channelling Mick' before capsizing the table. And poking me in
the eye. Anyway, no harm done. No permanent harm, at least.
By the way, I managed to record a snippet of you singing 'You
Were Always on My Mind' on my phone. Stirring stuff.

I'm a bit bewildered by your encounter with David in the
toilets, though. As indeed was he. Is it really Sally you're upset
about, or is there something you aren't admitting to yourself?

If it would make you feel any better, you can give me the

tambourine. See you tomorrow, and you can buy me lunch if you still feel bad. But there's really no need. I like you - but don't let it go to your head. Most people I like turn out to be complete idiots.

Lots of love,

Laura

PS. But please don't invite me to the theatre again. What was with that dancing jester? Sally and David were asking what I thought about the play on the way back. I said it was 'interesting' and 'thought-provoking'. I didn't reveal that the thought it mostly provoked was 'I hope the fire alarm goes off.' By the way, I've met them both before.

Part Four
Rock and Roll Heart

A Disciplinary Matter
The Ross Mystery Deepens
Betrayal • Underwear • Fork

A Disciplinary Matter

On Monday at 9:01 Martin Sergeant wrote:

Dear Martin Sargent,

We would appreciate it if you could come to room 13b
at 13:00 today. I will be there with Mr Simon Tapper from
Security. Please feel free to bring a colleague to act as a witness.
This is in relation to a security matter. I have copied this email
to Mr Tapper.

Yours sincerely,

Martin Sergeant, IT

On Monday at 9:04 Martin Sargent replied:

Right. And what's going to be in room 13b? A CD player with
'Ghostbusters' on it?

On Monday at 9:08 Martin Sergeant replied:

Dear Martin Sargent,

Our email monitoring system has detected an inappropriate
message sent from your work account, and we would like to
discuss it with you. Please be on time.

Yours sincerely,

Martin Sergeant, IT

On Monday at 9:12 Martin Sargent replied:

If this is about an email entitled 'Bosom Buddies', that was sent to me uninvited by a friend from school and I was forwarding it to show my disapproval.

On Monday at 9:15 Martin Sergeant replied:

Dear Mr Sargent,
We are aware of that correspondence, but this meeting is in relation to a separate and unrelated matter. As a general point the IT Department would like to underscore the point that work email should be used for work purposes only. We look forward to seeing you at 13:00.
     Yours sincerely,
        Martin Sergeant, IT

On Monday at 9:22 Martin Sargent wrote:

Barney (and whoever else is reading this)
Don't send me any more crap 'jokes' over the internet. I am in trouble at work about something to do with email misuse. Seriously.
Martin

On Monday at 9:33 Martin Sargent wrote:

Hi Laura
Thanks for your lovely email yesterday. I am afraid I may have to skip lunch today - see the attached from Martin Sergeant. He really does read our emails! Perhaps it's to do with my not wanting to live with him? God knows what all this is about. Tell you over lunch tomorrow? When you can also reveal how you've met David and Sally before.

Lots of Love
Martin

On Monday at 9:45 Laura replied:

Hi, Martin,

What have you been emailing? It wasn't that stupid 'Bosom Buddies' email, was it? You're in trouble with Martin Sergeant! Do you want me to get in touch with the union rep? I hear Martin can be a right batsard. Lunch tomorrow sounds fine - if you're still employed by this company by then.

Lots of love,

Laura

PS. I've checked who your union rep is - it's only Charlotte Greely. Things could get pretty messy in there. She threw Martin out of the flat again over the weekend.

On Monday at 9:48 Martin Sargent replied:

Again? Never realised the girlfriend was Charlotte 'the party at the Brewery is cancelled' Greely. Oh God, if she's thrown him out he's bound to be in a great mood today. And an even better one if he's reading this. I would like to make clear that I never thought he was gay, I like his glasses, and he is a fine young man. Why did his girlfriend throw him out (again)?

On Monday at 10:15 Laura replied:

Dunno. Perhaps because she found out that everyone in the office knew he'd been cheating on her with Kate Staple (again)? Good luck later - do you want me to come along?

On Monday at 10:20 Martin Sargent replied:

I think I can handle it alone. If I'm in there for more than about an hour, set off the fire alarm. Who is Simon Tapper?

On Monday at 10:22 Laura replied:

The grumpy little Security guy.

On Monday at 10:25 Martin Sargent replied:

Not that little guy who lurks around the lobby and shouts into his walkie-talkie? The one whose attitude screams 'three inches too short to get into the Prison Service'? We used to call him 'Ming the Merciless's little henchman'. He bloody hates me.

On Monday at 10:27 Laura replied:

Paranoid. Why would he hate you?

On Monday at 10:28 Martin Sargent replied:

Because he heard me refer to him as 'Ming the Merciless's little henchman'.

On Monday at 10:34 Laura replied:

Careful, I hear he has a bit of a short fuse. He's not inclined to be big about things like that. He thinks we all look down on him. He wants to do something more high-powered. He keeps his ear close to the ground. It's only a low-paid job, but he aspires to reach the heights of his profession.

On Monday at 10:35 Martin Sargent replied:

Does he feel dwarfed by his responsibilities?

\-

On Monday at 10:36 Laura replied:

Yes, but luckily he's got a great team working with him. Dorothy, the Tin Man, a Scarecrow, the Cowardly Lion, all the other Lollipop Men ...

\-

On Monday at 10:48 Martin Sargent replied:

Sorry for slow response. I had an email about work. I believe if things get really bad he can also call for back-up from Gandalf, Gimli and Galadriel.

\-

On Monday at 10:52 Laura replied:

So THAT'S why MediaSolutions has never been invaded by Orcs.

\-

On Monday at 10:53 Martin Sargent replied:

Yeah, and if things get really bad he can always get help from Val Kilmer.

\-

On Monday at 10:57 Laura replied:

?????

\-

On Monday at 10:58 Martin Sargent wrote:

Willow gag. With the sledge? And the pig?

On Monday at 11:05 Laura replied:

I think this has gone far enough. Please allow me to do some work, or I will report you to IT for misusing email. Good luck later. Word of advice: don't wear shoes with stacked heels.

On Monday at 12:38 Martin Sergeant wrote:

Dear Mr Sargent,
We would like to advise that a second disciplinary matter related to the misuse of email has now arisen, and will be discussed at our meeting today. Please be on time. Mr Tapper and I will see you in twenty minutes. Please wait outside room 13b until we call you in.
　　　Yours sincerely,
　　　　Martin Sergeant, IT

On Monday at 12:40 Martin Sargent replied:

Yes, yes, I'll be there shortly.

Jokes about Bombs

On Monday at 14:30 Martin Sergeant wrote:

Dear Mr Sargent,

Further to our meeting at 13:00 today in room 13b I am putting the following disciplinary complaints in written form, with the agreement of Mr Simon Tapper (Head of Security). Please print and retain a copy of this FORMAL WARNING. As you know the complaints are related to the misuse of MediaSolutions email and are as follows:

1) Using company email to encourage others to submit false bomb threats.

2) Using company email to encourage other to misuse fire alarms.

These are serious offences, and Mr Tapper and myself have made it clear that further violations will result in higher-level disciplinary proceedings. If you have any complaints regarding this procedure, please raise them with your union representative, Ms Charlotte Greely. At the present time Mr Tapper and I have decided against adding these infractions to your permanent record.

Jokes About Bombs Are Not Jokes.

Martin Sergeant, IT Department

Simon Tapper, Head of Security

On Monday at 14:31 Martin Sargent wrote:

Hi Laura

Have attached my warning from Tapper and Sergeant. Note their final comment. Surely that doesn't quite work? Surely

'Jokes About Bombs are Not Funny' or 'Jokes About Bombs Are No Joke' would be better?

I kept an admirably straight face when Tapper told me he'd have liked to 'take the matter higher'. Apparently (allegedly) it wasn't just Martin reading my emails: I used one of the 'trigger-words' that automatically raise an alert. I think a red light starts spinning on a computer in the IT room and a painting slides to one side to reveal a map of London with little flashing lights on. Then Martin uses a stick to push little(r) models of the security personnel around a big map on the table.

Jokes about Cub Scout's Woggles are Knot Jokes.
Martin

On Monday at 14:36 Laura wrote:

Al-Qaeda, jihad, George Bush
Martin Sergeant is a tool

On Monday at 14:37 Laura wrote:

Terror, Saudi link, mad mullah
Just testing, Martin.

On Monday at 14:40 Laura wrote:

It does work! I have to see Sergeant and Tapper tomorrow at lunch. Sandwiches on Wednesday?
                                                            Laura

PS. Hijack, Bliar, martyr
Martin Sergeant is a cheating batsard

George's Bush

On Monday at 16:23 Martin Sargent wrote:

Barney, you buttoncock, I'm not even going to open whatever crap it is you've sent me now. I have no interest in a jpeg entitled 'George's Bush'. Send it to my hotmail. This account is for work only.
Martin

P.S. Clash of civilisations, Rumsfeld, oil
Martin Sergeant sleeps under his desk in the office
P.P.S. Will explain when I next see you.

Bit of Consideration

Hi Martin,

Not being funny, mate, but did you leave the vacuum cleaner out? I tripped over it this morning and nearly broke my neck on the stairs. If you're looking for it later it's in my room because I was hoovering in there earlier - feel free to go in and get it.

Ross

PS Would be great if you could pick up some milk for the morning on your way back from work. I'll probably be back late.

The Inner Sanctum

On Monday at 20:34 Martin wrote:

Hi Lucy

Today gets odder and odder. I've just been inside Ross's room for the first time since he moved in. I wasn't spying, I went in to get the hoover (to quote Mum). Well, that clears up where the smell was coming from. And where all the cutlery went to. Christ, not even a badger fouls its own lair. I went to let some air in and there was a pubic hair stuck right to the middle of the window. How? Why? I trod in a bloody tuna sandwich in bare feet as well. I swear to God there was a dried-out slice of cucumber on Ross's pillow. Perhaps he was saving it for the morning? A touch of class: he claims to have vacuumed in there today, but the floor is still covered in clothes. Conclusion? He did the bachelor classic of hovering *round* the piles of crapola on the floor. The whole room smelled like when you leave damp sports kit in the hall all holidays and open it the day before the start of term to find it's grown mushrooms. No wonder he's always out. That's another thing - where does he go? Not buying milk, that's for damn sure. And if he's really serious about being a writer, where is his *Writers' and Artists' Yearbook*?
Lots of Love
Martin

On Tuesday at 11:20 Lucy replied:

Gross. That's really helped my hangover. Must go and puke now before lectures. Speak soon.

113

Re: A Disciplinary Matter

On Tuesday at 12:00 Laura wrote:

Why is the union so utterly useless? Bloody Charlotte
Greely has got back to me to say she can't come with me to my
disciplinary meeting. No excuse offered. Not even: I don't want
to see my on-off boyfriend and so I am being wet. Then again
you have to wonder about someone who volunteers to be union
rep anyway. The rumour is she went for it because she was
pissed off that Julie was made First Aid Officer. And she wasn't
made milk monitor at school and that still stings.

On Tuesday at 12:32 Martin replied:

I'll come along to support if you want. I hope you're not
wearing high heels. I think Petty Officer Tapper is actually
shrinking.

On Tuesday at 12:41 Laura replied:

He's being eaten up with rage. Perhaps he thinks we all look
down our noses at him?

On Tuesday at 12:42 Martin replied:

Oh God, don't start that again. He'll never reach the top with
that kind of altitude. Sorry, that should read 'attitude'.
On a related note, do you know Craig, otherwise known as

the nice security guard? i.e. the one who will actually hold a door if you are carrying a box of stationery, and who smiles when you come in, and doesn't generally act as if his job would be a lot easier if people didn't insist on getting in the way by trying to use the building as an office? He came up to me this morning and said he'd heard I'd had a run-in with 'Toulouse-la-twat'. Apparently all the cleaning staff hate him too. He asked Benita why she didn't wear a burqa. Ummm, is it because she's Peruvian? But under what possible combination of circumstances would you ask someone that, anyway? She's the coolest cleaner by a long way. Have you noticed she NEVER takes her rings off ever?

Why didn't you volunteer to be union rep? People actually like and respect you...

On Tuesday at 12:45 Laura replied:

Sweet of you to say, but I do know that. I bloody should be union rep. WHY is the coffee machine still broken? And how come all the best magazines end up in the smoking room? And which practical joker hired the receptionist with the speech impediment?

Come along at one - it's in room 13b again. Otherwise known as the Security sandwich room. That's why the meeting can't go on beyond one thirty - they all want to come in and have their lunch.

On Tuesday at 12:46 Martin replied:

I don't think it's a speech impediment. I think she talks like that because she's deaf. See you at the sandwich room. I mean anti-terror nerve centre.

Judas

Tee hee no written warning for me.

On Tuesday at 14:03 Martin replied:

I can't believe you sold me out.

On Tuesday at 14:12 Laura replied:

Well, you have been getting a bit smug. I said the contact lens incident was forgotten, not forgiven.

On Tuesday at 14:15 Martin replied:

I'm going to complain to the union.

On Tuesday at 14:18 Laura replied:

Well, how do you know I wasn't telling the truth? I might have got the spellings of your surnames mixed up and been calling you a tool. The look of triumph on Tapper's face when I said that. I made his day.

On Tuesday at 14:19 Martin replied:

You made his life. As for the implication that you were acting as an agent provocateur and trying to trick me into revealing my terrorist sympathies...

On Tuesday at 14:25 Laura replied:

Yes, I wondered if that was over-egging it. I got a very strange look from Martin when I said 'agent provocateur'. The thought of Charlotte Greely in expensive lingerie is a bit much for a Tuesday lunchtime, I must say.

On Tuesday at 14:26 Martin replied:

Tomorrow for the long-delayed lunch, then? Of course, that's provided they let me back into the building...

By the way, the best magazines end up in the smoking room because that's where the cool kids hang out. You should come on down sometime and join the emphasemic bitching. You've not lived until you've heard Benita dissect a copy of *Hello!* over a Rothman's: ' 'e is a gay' (turns page), 'e is a gay (turns page), I can't believe she is marryin' 'im, 'e is a gay and all (throws paper down in disgust, lights up again).' She literally never makes any other comment. She was next to me the other day, and she pointed at a picture of Elton, and said, 'An' 'e is the biggest gay of the lot.' I couldn't think of an adequate response.

On Tuesday at 14:31 Laura replied:

Did she mean by campitude or by sheer body mass, I wonder. Or perhaps she's trying to tell you something?

PS. You're the one to be funny about other people's accents. Your voice goes really posh when you're plastered. 'Hands orf my tambourine'.

Simple Maths

On Wednesday at 14:15 Martin wrote:

Hey Ella

I had a very interesting conversation over lunch with someone
who saw David and Sally snogging outrageously at a party
nine weeks ago. Apparently they almost fell out of a window.
Apparently they didn't even stop kissing to drink, and were
pouring white wine out of a single glass into the gap left between
their two sets of slobbering lips. Apparently Sally was sitting on
his lap with her skirt rolling up and ruffling his horrible orange
hair. Apparently no one could get to their coats at the end of
the evening, because they'd locked themselves in the cloakroom.
I don't have orange hair, and I don't drink white wine, so I
don't think it's a case of mistaken identity. Now I'm not Carol
Vorderman, but nine weeks ago Sally still lived with me. In fact,
nine weeks ago I was at a stag weekend in Wales. Now I was a
bit sleepy when I got back, but I think I would have remembered
if Sally mentioned snogging someone. Particularly if she'd told
me she almost rolled out of a window doing so.

I can only assume that you knew about this? Does everyone?
I'd appreciate it if you would put me out of my misery.
Martin

P.S. And it was a shit stag weekend. Since when did people start
going go-karting and sleeping out in tents to celebrate the end of
their bachelorhood?

On Wednesday at 14:30 Ella replied:

Hi, Martin

By 'put you out of your misery', I guess you mean tell you what I know about Sally and David. As opposed to shooting you like a broken pony. I assumed Sally told you when she moved out. That was why I wanted to avoid being at the first night of the play. But if you didn't know why have you been making such a total cocksneeze of yourself? Jesus - you broke his nose and you didn't know he'd been shagging Sally behind your back?

Well, yes, that party was the first time they got together. If you think it's been tough on you, I've had to hear Sally dripping on about it for nine weeks in the way only actresses can. She's been very confused, she had strong feelings for both of you, David was overwhelmingly attractive and brilliant, the sex was amazing, etc, etc. Imagine my surprise when I first met this astonishing prodigy and found he was a loathsome little goblin. Obviously I feel pretty bad about not telling you, but then I'm Sally's mate too and I hoped it wouldn't come to this. She didn't mention his hideous tapered combat trousers, otherwise I would have been much firmer about telling her to stick with you.

Did 'everyone' know? No. I knew, all Sally's other friends knew, and a sizeable selection of yours as well. But the vast majority of the world went on with their daily routine unaware of the seismic events unfolding in north-west London. I know it's a shock and all, but please keep it in proportion. After all, you knew they're together now, so is it really such a big deal that they got together then? It could have been one of those things that make someone realise how much they treasure what they have. Unfortunately, it wasn't. So yes, we knew, but we didn't go dancing around with models of you with horns, shouting 'cuckoo', 'cuckoo'. Well, we did actually, but that was for kicks, not out of malice. No one refers to you as 'Martin the Cuckold'. Possibly because we don't know any other Martins.

In fact, had one of your friends come to you under similar circumstances, you would have done exactly the same thing. I'd say it's a chance for you both to grow and move on in your lives, but let's be honest, the whole thing will probably gnaw at you in the night for years and shrivel you up inside 'til you're a wizened drunk muttering about never trusting women in a pub that you haven't noticed has been remodelled as a theme bar. Or you end up wandering around Oxford Circus asking people if they're a winner or a sinner.

Let's face it, when the sex goes you're just friends. And friends who bicker all the time aren't very good for each other. Hope this helps.

Ella

PS (In response to your PS) I don't know when that happened. Moreover, I don't care. Blame it on feminism and get your own opinion column in the *Daily Mail*.
PPS I was alarmed to see that Carol Vorderman is the only mathematician you know the name of.

On Wednesday at 14:40 Martin replied:

Thanks, Ella, for your borderline-autistic candour. And thanks for the revelation that they were actually having sex, too. I thought I was upset when I was just imagining heavy petting.

I don't follow your argument about the timing. That's like saying 'well, yes, it was murder, but the victim's dead now anyway, so it doesn't really matter.'

And, by the way, the sex hadn't gone.
Martin

On Wednesday at 14:42 Ella replied:

Umm, I think when you turn down the offer of lovemaking with your partner in order to watch a documentary about Lou Reed, the sex has gone.

On Wednesday at 14:43 Martin replied:

Oh come on! I can't believe she told you that. They hardly ever show *Rock and Roll Heart*, and I offered to put a video in.

On Wednesday at 14:46 Ella replied:

When you turn down sex with your beautiful and sexy partner to watch someone with a mullet and no end on his guitar doing songs from *Magic and Loss*, while one of Penn and Teller talks about how much the *New York* album means to him, the sparkle has left the bedroom. And for God's sake, you don't say 'Let's do it on the counter' when someone is trying to cook lunch for your parents.

God it feels good to finally be able to tell you these things.

On Wednesday at 14:48 Martin replied:

You are a cold cold person, Ella.

On Wednesday at 14:52 Ella replied:

Yes I am. But for fuck's sake I can't stand all this moping and mewling about. And that goes for the pair of you, but particularly you. Why act as if you're going to challenge David to a duel when the worst it will ever come to is you giving his plays anonymous bad reviews online? A couple of tearful wanks and you'll be fine.

And for goodness' sake if you're going to liven things up by having sex in the woods a) at least one of you should preferably be wearing a skirt and b) make sure you tie the dog up securely. I'd love to have been a fly on the wall that weekend: 'So how did Digger get loose in the first place, Martin?' 'Well, the thing was, Mr Kendle, I was trying to boff your daughter and we couldn't

122

work out what to do with her jeans.' 'One leg off, boy, one leg off.'

I think you should give Sally her underwear back, too.
Warm regards, Ella

On Wednesday at 15:03 Martin replied:

Trust me, she wouldn't want it back now. By the way, this may be totally inappropriate, but I'm sure I could recover a lot of my sex confidence if I was to practise with someone who I didn't feel too strongly about and who I knew wasn't going to get all hung up on me.
Martin

On Wednesday at 15:04 Ella replied:

You couldn't begin to handle me, Sargent.

Just a Pint

On Wednesday at 20:15 Martin wrote:

By the way I was joking about the underwear.

On Thursday at 10:10 Ella replied:

So I assumed. Until I got this email.

On Thursday at 10:11 Martin replied:

I was joking about the other thing, too.

On Thursday at 10:15 Ella replied:

Oh damn. But wasn't it Freud who said there's no such thing as a joke?

On Thursday at 10:16 Martin replied:

I think he said there's no such thing as an accident, actually.

On Thursday at 10:18 Ella replied:

Nice try, though. Pint next week?

On Thursday at 10:22 Martin replied:

Ah, but surely there's no such thing as a pint...

Yesterday

On Thursday at 10:35 Laura wrote:

Dear Martin,

I'm really sorry if what I told you upset you yesterday. I guess that story's a lot less funny if one of the people involved is your ex. It was very inconsiderate of me.

I don't know if I should mention this, but it seems relevant that the person who turned up at mine unannounced last weekend was Gwyn, my ex. He unloaded a lot of stuff on me (emotional stuff) and is in quite a bad way, so I'm not really sure what to do about that at the moment. Anyway, doubt it makes much difference, but I wanted you to know.

Lots of love

Laura

On Thursday at 10:50 Martin replied:

The ex in the band?

On Thursday at 11:15 Laura replied:

Yeah, but they've broken up. That was part of what he was so upset about. Except they haven't actually broken up. They told him they had, and then he rang the drummer up for a pint and found they were on tour in Belgium and Germany with a new singer. He was talking about getting back together, which has taken me a bit by surprise. (Getting back together with me, not with Fork).

126

On Thursday at 11:22 Martin replied:

Your ex's band is called Fork? That's aggressively bland. I suppose Spoon was already taken. I can imagine the scene: they were all at dinner, trying to choose a name… May I hazard a guess they are a knock-kneed indie guitar band? Does he wear a jacket with badges on the lapels?

On Thursday at 11:32 Laura replied:

Afraid so. They used to be called The Romantic Movement, so Fork is an improvement.

He was in a state, actually, so I kind of felt I had to let him stay for a bit. He's being quite sweet - he's written some really good new songs about how things have been for him.

On Thursday at 11:35 Martin replied:

How nice of him. This is the boyfriend who owes you money?

On Thursday at 11:52 Laura replied:

Not very much money.

On Thursday at 11:53 Martin replied:

This is the ex-boyfriend, to be clear, who has the attractive habits of scratching his crotch and blowing his nose into his palm and then chucking it?

On Thursday at 11:55 Laura replied:

Look, I was very upset when I told you that. I don't think you should judge until you've met him.

On Thursday at 11:57 Martin replied:

I can't wait. This is the guy who your friends refused to let in the house after he threatened your neighbour with a hammer?

On Thursday at 12:00 Laura replied:

Well, he's very protective, and the neighbour used to peer in the windows.

On Thursday at 12:01 Martin replied:

There's such a fine line between psychotic and protective. Oh, wait a minute, actually there isn't. You said the neighbour was about 80.

On Thursday at 12:05 Laura replied:

Not more than 60. Besides, Gwyn was going through a stormy patch with the label.

On Thursday at 12:06 Martin replied:

I don't suppose it's any of my business. What's he going to do now? Start up a hardware shop?

On Thursday at 12:17 Laura replied:

Well, for the moment he's staying at mine.

On Thursday at 12:20 Martin wrote:

Hi Lucy
How are you? Aaaaaaaaaaaaaaaaaaaaaaargh! Bollocks! Women
are idiots! Men are idiots! Hope things are going well with the
boy Sam. Speak soon.
Lots of Love
Martin

On Thursday at 12:58 Lucy replied:

Feel better, mate? Of course they are. Otherwise no one would
ever get together and the race would die out. Everything going
well with Laura?
    Lots of love,
    Lucy
    PS: Going to the pictures tonight, but speak at weekend.

On Thursday at 13:03 Martin wrote:

Hey Laura
Hope that works out. Do you fancy a spot of lunch in a mo?
Martin

On Thursday at 14:23 Laura replied:

Hi Martin,
Sorry I missed your email. Had to meet Gwyn for sandwiches
and to look at some instruments. Took a bit longer than expected

and only just snuck back in. Hope you didn't have a lonely lunchbreak!

    Lots of love,

Laura

Part Five

DJ Idiot and the Adventures of the Dialectic

If I Had a Hammer ...

On Thursday at 14:45 Martin wrote:

Hi Barney
Thanks for your help piecing together the shattered fragments of last Thursday night. No one seems inclined to prosecute, thank god. Ross and I are in negotiations over who gets custody of the tambourine, so I can't comment on that at the moment. Could I ask you a favour? I'm putting together a themed collection of songs for someone - do you have any of the following?: 'If I had a Hammer', 'Maxwell's Silver Hammer', anything by MC Hammer; any Hammer Horror themes...
Cheers
Martin

On Thursday at 15:20 Barney replied:

Alright squire,
I've got a bootleg which mixes 'Hammer Time' with 'Don't Stop' by Fleetwood Mac. Any good to you?
Keep it loose, Bruce,
Barney

On Thursday at 15:23 Martin replied:

That's perfect. Presumably it's called 'Don't Stop Thinking about Hammer Time'?

On Thursday at 15:33 Barney replied:

Nah - 'Hammer Time'll Soon Be Here'. Actually, I'm making one that mixes 'Hammer Time' with 'Immigrant Song' by Led Zeppelin.

On Thursday at 15:34 Martin replied:

'Hammer Time of the Gods?'
By the way, surely you're meant to be at work?
Hope all well.

On Thursday at 15:40 Barney replied:

I am at work. I'm smiling at one of the partners across the office as we speak. I'm an artist, Martin. I can't just turn it off. Titlewise, I was thinking of 'Led Zep please don't hurt 'em'.
All going extremely well with me - hooked up with someone after the gallery party. I believe you know her, a girl called Ella? We had a long chat about you, in fact.

On Thursday at 15:42 Martin replied:

I can imagine exactly what you were discussing.
Stop.
Hammer Time.
You hooked up with Ella Tvertko?

On Thursday at 15:43 Martin wrote:

Sorry, I forgot that emails don't always convey the proper emphasis: *You* hooked up with *Ella Tvertko*? She whose icy beauty freezes Evian at twenty paces?

On Thursday at 15:47 Barney replied:

Yes, *I* hooked up with (i.e. spent the night with (i.e. to put it bluntly, shagged)) Ella Tvertko. Seeing her again tonight in fact, after the play. Shall I send my regards?

On Thursday at 15:48 Martin replied:

Send my outraged jealousy. You shagged Ella Tvertko. But how?

On Thursday at 15:49 Martin wrote:

To clarify that last bit: how did you end up pulling her?

On Thursday at 15:51 Barney replied:

Actually, she pulled me. Like I said, it's not something I can turn off. Oh and by the way, it was astonishing. Sorry, that should read *astonishing*.

On Thursday at 15:53 Martin replied:

Well, farewell, Old Mate. She will devour you. There will be nothing left of you but a pair of headphones and an 'ironic' wristband. And perhaps the lingering whiff of unutterable smugness.

On Thursday at 15:54 Barney replied:

Counting on it, mate, counting on it. Jealous much?

On Thursday at 15:55 Martin wrote:

Hi Laura

Don't suppose you saw a cheap pair of record decks for sale when you were out at lunchtime? It seems the years I have spent trying to attract girls by transforming myself into a sensitive, charming, well-informed and fully rounded human being have been a total waste of time. What I really should have been doing is practising how to play two records at once while wearing a silly pair of sunglasses.

Martin

Re: DJ Idiot

On Thursday at 16:04 Martin wrote:

Well, well, Ella. I hear you hooked up with DJ Idiot last night. One question: why? Free drink, was it? Oh sorry, two questions. Yours in disbelief
Martin

On Thursday at 16:45 Ella wrote:

Hey, Martin
Simple answer: He's sexy. Nice strong chin. Getting ready to see him later. Lucky boy. Should give me something to think about during this bloody play, anyhow. Nice to see what loyal mates Mark has.
Ella

On Thursday at 16:47 Martin replied:

I know he's my mate, but he's also a complete foolio. He makes Dr Fox look like Merleau-Ponty. And he's rubbish at DJing. He's totally undeserving.
Martin

On Thursday at 16:52 Ella replied:

Poor sweet Martin,
It's got nothing to do with being deserving - it doesn't work

like AirMiles, you know. Do I really have to explain this to you? I'm not putting together a pub quiz team.

On Thursday at 16:53 Martin replied:

Just as well. He once told me: 'You can knock Cathy Dennis all you want, but she did write "Waterloo Sunset"'.

On Thursday at 16:57 Ella replied:

So what?

On Thursday at 16:58 Martin replied:

So it's by Ray Davies. Everyone knows that! It was a wretched cover version as well.

On Thursday at 17:02 Ella replied:

Well done. You've proved whatever minor point you wanted to make. By the way, this is all a bit creepy of you. It's really none of your business, panty-hoarder.

On which note, you know Mark pretty well: thong or something more sensible?

On Thursday at 17:05 Martin replied:

Point taken, point taken. As for the pants, I don't care and I never want to know. Just don't break him - he's my idiot and he has sentimental value.

Big News

On Thursday at 18:22 Emily wrote:

Hi Martin

Hope the play was good. Sorry we missed it (No we're not
- Chris. Oops and we missed it again last night as well. Sorry,
Sally). Apologies, Chris is reading this over my shoulder. How
about a good, honest pint on Friday? We've got big news!

Emily (and Chris)

PS. To make things clear, Chris and I have discussed this and
are in total agreement. We will meet in a pub. A normal pub.
To drink pints or perhaps a glass or two of wine. Like normal
people. At no point in the evening will you reveal that you have
taken us to the most haunted pub in London, or Lord Lucan's old
local, or anything involving bloody Dickens. If we're hungry we
may order Twiglets or a bag of crinkle-cut crisps. There will be
no eels, no roasted trotters and certainly no winkles. And if you
use the word 'psychogeography' or let slip that we are drinking
in an establishment built on the site of Pepys's old house or
Black Bess's stable or a plague pit, I will glass you myself. Or
should I say, invite you to partake in the timeless violence of this
most unpredictable of cities ...

On Thursday at 18:45 Martin replied:

Can't interest you in a night of avant-garde burlesque in
Clapham?

On Thursday at 19:23 Emily replied:

Hi Martin,

Chris here. Using Emily's email account in a spirit of
transgressive subversion of which I trust you will approve. We
have thought seriously about your offer of a night in Clapham
watching burlesque, and have decided against. Instead, I am
going to soak my balls in white spirit and then Emily is going
to flick matches at me. I hope this answers your question. Come
for a pint. Will text to arrange shortly. Don't make any more
suggestions that we all do something else 'cultural' and tedious or
I will kill you. I'm not joking.

Chris

Fork Is Genius!

On Thursday at 21:25 Johannes wrote:

Dear Gwyn

I can't believe I am writing to you. I am biggest fan of Fork from Dusseldorf. Before I liked The Doors and Pink Floyd but now Fork is my favourite. You are so great! I have all your record and even poster and my mother made me T-shirt with Fork on. But when I wear it to your gig last night I am so disappointed because there was new singer. He is not so great! I want you to rejoin band. You are the best singer. I write to band as well, and tell them new singer 'sucks'. You should rejoin Fork and make more brilliant indie guitar music with them. Perhaps you should tour Australia and the Far East for a long time.

Yours truly

Johannes Jester

Your Idiot

On Friday at 12:06 Barney wrote:

Who is Merlot-Poncy?

On Friday at 12:23 Martin wrote:

Maurice Merleau-Ponty (1908-1961)

A key figure in post-war French philosophy. Merleau-Ponty
served in the infantry during the Second World War, and in 1949
was appointed to the chair of Child Psychology at the Sorbonne. In
1952 he became the youngest person ever appointed to the chair of
Philosophy at the College de France. In 1945 he co-founded with
Jean-Paul Sartre and Simone de Beauvoir the influential political,
literary and philosophical journal *Les Temps modernes*. Like Sartre
and de Beauvoir, Merleau-Ponty is usually associated with the
existentialist movement, although he remained sceptical of some of
the movement's more extreme accounts of personal freedom and
responsibility. Indeed, Merleau-Ponty extensively critiqued many
of Sartre's positions, not least what he saw as the privileging
of subject-object relations in Sartre's version of
phenomenology. Merleau-Ponty's disagreements with many of
Sartre's political positions was also a key factor in the somewhat
bitter ending of their friendship. Merleau-Ponty gave his
assessment of their differences in *Adventures of the Dialectic*, while
Sartre's version of events is recounted in *Situations*. Merleau-
Ponty died before completing his final work, *The Visible and
the Invisible*, which was to have been both a rethinking and an
extension of his attempts throughout his philosophical career to
break down the traditional dualisms between sensibility and
understanding, activity and passivity, mind and body.

<u>Dr Fox (1961-)</u>

Actual name: Neil Fox. Also known as 'Foxy'. Should not be confused with Dr Liam Fox, Conservative MP.

Dr Fox began his radio career as a student, broadcasting under the name Andrew Howe on University Radio Bath. After graduating Foxy worked for a time selling printed plastic bags, before getting a job on Radio Wyvern (97.6 FM in Herefordshire, 102.8 FM in Worcestershire). In less than a year he had been signed up to work on Radio Luxembourg. From 1987 until 2005 he was a presenter with Capital Radio. He also fronted Channel 5's Pepsi Chart Show from 1998 to 2002, alongside the greatly underrated Liz Eastwood. He is probably best known as the indulgent judge on the TV talent show *Pop Idol*. Fact: He's not really a doctor, but he does have a degree in Business and Marketing. His work's relationship to that of Jean-Paul Sartre remains hotly debated.

On Friday at 12:25 Barney replied:

To quote Merleau-Ponty's *Adventures of the Dialectic*: 'Vous êtes un cul'.

Need a translation?

On Friday at 12:27 Martin replied:

Mme Deganis would be so proud. Only trying to save you from getting hurt, mate.

On Friday at 12:29 Barney replied:

Cheers pal. (Since emails don't always convey tone I should explain that the previous phrase is to be delivered in a tone of withering sarcasm). I think I know exactly what you were trying to 'save' me from.

Last Night

On Friday at 12:30 Sally wrote:

Dear Martin,
I don't think it's a very good idea if you ring me drunk again. Or indeed at all, if you're going to be like this. I'm not going to apologise for falling in love with someone else, and I think it's rather selfish of you to expect me to.
    Sally

On Friday at 12:34 Martin replied:

Oh come on now, Sally,
I thought it was easy to apologise but hard to accept an apology. Try me.
Love
Martin

On Friday at 12:40 Sally replied:

What am I supposed to be apologising for?

On Friday at 12:45 Martin replied:

Oh, I don't know...
Oh yes I do. How about hooking up with the Phantom of the Pub Theatre behind my back? Several weeks behind my back. And then leaving me sitting around thinking things were all

my fault and you moving out was something to do with me not cleaning the oven or forgetting your pony's birthday?
Martin

On Friday at 12:50 Sally replied:

Are you still drunk?

On Friday at 12:51 Martin replied:

I may have had a pint at lunch.

On Friday at 12:54 Sally replied:

It's only 12:54.

On Friday at 12:55 Martin replied:

Breakfast, then.

On Friday at 13:04 Sally replied:

Please don't get in touch with me until you're prepared to be reasonable about what has happened. I have bent over backwards to make this whole thing amicable, but you seem determined to make everything as unpleasant as you can. I think, when you look at things soberly, you will realise you are being an ass.

On Friday at 13:09 Martin replied:

Well I have a right to be an ass. I'm an ass and proud. I'm

a cuckolded ass and I'm bad at sex. But I'm a free ass in giddy London.

On Friday at 13:13 Martin wrote:

Hi Laura

Lunch? I've spilled something on my computer and I have to get out of here. Meet me at the Grapes in three minutes. It's Friday! Pub lunch on me! Also meeting up with mates later if you want to come too. Gwyn not invited - planning on getting hammered, but not literally.

Martin the Ass

Wallet

On Saturday at 9:58 Martin wrote:

Hi Chris

Many congratulations again on your big news. I had a great night. I have big news of my own, in fact: I don't suppose you saw what I did with my tie, jacket or indeed wallet? Presumably I had at least one of them in the taxi. Unless I drunkenly blew the driver for a free ride. Again. Couldn't have a fouler tasting mouth this morning if I had.

Yuck.

Martin

P.S. So I assume the obvious...?

P.P.S. Seriously mate, she's a lovely girl. God knows what she sees in you.

On Saturday at 10:45 Chris replied:

Not sure what happened to your stuff, mate. Don't think you left it in the pub. I can assure you we haven't nicked your wallet to defray the cost of the wedding. No, Emily is not with child, if that is 'the obvious'. Cheeky bastard. As it happens we've been on the waiting-list for the chapel for quite a while. They've had an unexpected cancellation for later in the year, so it's all going to be a bit of a rush.

On Saturday at 11:00 Martin wrote:

Emily

It's not too late to back out. I'll always wait for you. We can even raise the child as our own, and live in the mountains.

On Saturday at 11:32 Emily replied:

Martin, you know I use this account as well. I hope the offer stands for me too? I think lederhosen would quite suit me, in fact, and I can see you in a little Tiroler hat. Trust me, if Emily really was knocked up, I'd be holding a goat on a glacier before you could say 'yodel-eei-hoo'.

Chris

On Saturday at 11:40 Martin replied:

By the way, I don't suppose you've had a chance to think about potential best men? This is an enquiry, not a hint...

Re: Wallet

On Saturday at 11:47 Laura wrote:

Dear Martin 'the Ass'

Didn't make it into work yesterday due to crisis at home. Sorry to stand you up! Hope the Grapes was OK. Isn't it a bit grim? Whenever I've been in it's full of shaky old men with watery eyes. How was the night out with your friends?

Laura

On Saturday at 12:56 Martin replied:

Hi Laura

Yes, it is an extraordinarily depressing place for a solitary lunchtime pint.

Gosh, I feel terrible. My mates announced their engagement last night, and the toasting went on into the early hours. I seem to have lost my jacket and tie. And wallet. But not, for once, my dignity.

I've had to ring round and cancel all my cards. Waiting for my flatmate to come home and hopefully buy me some food.

On Saturday at 13:20 Laura replied:

Oh, in that case you are an ass. What did you spill on your computer?

PS. I don't really think you're an ass. I know worse.

On Saturday at 14:01 Martin replied:

Ribena. I think I was trying to make a cocktail...
I've found my jacket in the kitchen. My wallet was on the
sideboard with all cards present and correct. But of course
they're all now cancelled so entirely useless. Still, if I get really
hungry there's some lettuce and a little fragment of kebab meat
in one of the jacket pockets. There's no sign of my tie, though.
Or my flatmate.

On Saturday at 14:12 Laura replied:

How annoying. If you can scrape together enough for a travel
card you can come over here for dinner later. I might even be
persuaded to take you out for a pizza.

On Saturday at 14:15 Martin replied:

Sounds great. But won't Gwyn mind? I would prefer not to be
hit with a hammer.

On Saturday at 14:21 Laura replied:

Nah, he's rehearsing tonight and staying with mates
afterwards. We had a bit of a row yesterday morning. Would
be lovely to see you. Come over. But we must try to figure out
where your tie is, using logical deduction from the available
evidence. First, eliminate the obvious. Are you wearing it?

On Saturday at 14:22 Martin replied:

Aha!... No.

On Saturday at 14:23 Laura replied:

Nope, it's no good, it's lost. You'll have to hire a psychic. Haven't you got another one you could wear on Monday?

On Saturday at 14:26 Martin replied:

I've got a tie Dad gave me for Christmas, but I don't know if it really projects the right image for work. It's got Homer Simpson on with a can of beer, and he's thinking 'Hmmm Beer'. I don't even think it's official. Homer looks a bit orange and his head is slightly rectangular. Cheers, Pop. Oh God, I'm much too hungover today to start contemplating the sadness of dadness.

On Saturday at 14:31 Laura replied:

Well, it's the thought that counts - although I'm not sure that saying is very reassuring in this context. Wear it on Monday!
On a similar note, last birthday Gwyn gave me a load of cheesy lingerie and a spice rack. Pretty subtle demonstration of how he thinks about me. And he gave me that card with a skinhead saying to an old granny 'Show us yer tits'. And inside the card she lifts up her skirt and there they are, dangling around her knees. That was just before we broke up, in fact ...

On Saturday at 14:35 Martin replied:

Charming. I always wondered in what possible circumstances that card would be appropriate. Guess I'll have to keep on wondering.
I got the birthday tie out to have a look at and it's brought the sadness. It's the thought of Dad seeing it and thinking, 'Martin likes *The Simpsons* and he drinks beer, this is the perfect present'.

On Saturday at 14:37 Laura replied:

I think perhaps we need to get you a new tie ...
Actually, to be fair, it is a bloody nice spice rack.

Change of Plans

On Saturday at 18:02 Laura wrote:

Hi, Martin,

Sorry about this, but can we do the pizza another night? I tried to call you, but the phone was engaged, so I guess you're online. Gwyn has reappeared after all and I get the feeling we're going to have to have yet another discussion about 'us'. I feel rubbish about this, but I hope you'll understand. Hope your flatmate comes back to feed you! So sorry to muck you about, and I would much much rather be having pizza with you. Good luck with the tie hunt, and look forward to seeing you on Monday.

Lots of love

Laura

Re: Fork Is Genius!

On Sunday at 15:26 Gwyn wrote:

Dear Johanna.

Thank you for your lovely email. It was really nice to hear from a fan. But I'm afraid to say Fork have broken up, and we won't be working together any more. Don't worry - we are still great friends and I wish them all the greatest success with their new singer. Although you're right, he's not as good as me!!!

Anyhow, I am working with a new band now, and we will be doing new material as well as favourites from the Fork days. We are rehearsing at the moment and we are called Acklington Stanley. Our first gig is in London in a few weeks and I hope we will be touring Germany soon. Not sure about the Far East but anything is possible!!!

I'll be looking forward to meeting you.

Gwyn

Neglected

On Sunday at 16:01 Martin wrote:

Hello Sis
Remember me? We used to email each other. Presumably
things going well with Sam. Not going home for the holidays?
Lots of Love
Martin
(your brother)

Review

On Sunday at 16:04 Martin wrote:

Hi Sally

Guess what? I'm emailing to apologise. I shouldn't have rung you drunk, and I'm now prepared to act like a human being. I saw the online review - congratulations. By the way, Chris and Emily are getting married. They said they'd love it if we both came to the wedding. I hope that wouldn't be too weird for you. Anyway, look forward to hearing all your news. Regards to David.

Best

Martin

On Sunday at 16:09 Martin wrote:

Hi Laura

I've been reading an online review of *The Lady of Shalott*. Unbelievably, they thought it showed promise. I quote: 'As I crammed into the New Place with the rest of the hipsters and theatre in-crowd I was prepared to dislike David Fauntleroy's new reading of *The Lady of Shalott*. Partly improvised? Live DJ? Dancing onstage? All the signs were there for a thoroughly self-indulgent evening.'

(So far so good, but wait...)

'But I am pleased to report that David Fauntleroy has given this hoariest of ideas new clothes, and they look... pretty fine, actually. With a gifted cast and a willingness to push any envelope he encounters, Fauntleroy conjures a magical evening out of the air with all the confidence and talent of a new Merlin (if that's not mixing my Arthurian legends!).'

And so on, and so on, before concluding: 'In particular the use of mime, particularly at the finale, and the playful use of music made this an evening I would recommend to anyone who is still prepared to believe in theatrical magic. Deserves a bigger space. Five Stars.'

Who is Danny Rodham? Has too much theatre driven him insane? Did he actually go to the play? There's a little box at the bottom of the page where you can add your own opinion. One can only hope that the general public takes full advantage of this opportunity.

Perhaps we are just philistines.

Hope last night was OK. Ross appeared eventually and brought me some chips, and I found a scotch egg in the fridge.
Lots of Love
Martin

On Sunday at 17:12 Laura replied:

Hmmm, mysterious. But it depends how many stars he has to give. Perhaps it's five out of a hundred. What bigger space has he in mind? Perhaps a transfer to the Arctic tundra could be arranged.

What is 'pushing the envelope'? It sounds painful.

So sorry to let you down last night. Gwyn and I managed to have a pretty good talk, though. I let him know my disapproval of his choice in birthday presents. Hope your scotch egg was nice.

Glad to hear we are hipsters.
Lots of love,

Laura

Quick Query

On Sunday at 17:16 Martin wrote:

Hey Barney

Are you still PO'd at me? I don't suppose you know where I could hire a hitman, preferably one who can do a job-lot at discount prices? Axe, garrotte, rifle, I don't mind as long as they're good.

Otherwise, and unless you're busy, pint later?

Martin

On Sunday at 18:19 Barney replied:

Too knackered and drained of essential vitamins to bear a grudge. Not sure about hitmen, but will ask around. Would love to come for pint but can't speak - I think I tore that little piece of skin underneath my tongue. Also can't walk. And I'm typing this with my nose. I may never DJ again.

On Sunday at 18:42 Martin replied:

I'll withhold comment regarding your DJing. No need to rub it in, mate. Glad you're having fun.

On Sunday at 18:45 Barney replied:

It's gone beyond fun, mate. It's either love or at some point soon Ella is going to bite my head off and lay her eggs in my torso.

PS Don't suppose Chris needs a DJ for the wedding?

On Sunday at 18:52 Martin replied:

He didn't mention it, but I'll put in the good word.

PS Barney, by the way, I was joking about the hitman.

Re: Review

On Sunday at 19:14 Ella wrote:

Martin,
Have you seen the online review of that awful play of Sally's?
Ella

On Sunday at 19:16 Martin replied:

I know, the world has gone mad. Rodham must be another victim of David's drugged bread. The idea that that clown pushes any sort of envelope is an insult to postal workers everywhere.

On Sunday at 19:18 Ella replied:

I added my own comment to the general melee on the messageboard. At least we're not alone in our opinion. See if you can guess which one was mine. I take it 'My favourite bit was the bloke who wandered in and wanted cigarettes, the rest was mad gay' is your handiwork? I didn't think you were going to take me literally about slagging David off anonymously online. It's so creepy of you. Not that I entirely disapprove.
Ella

On Sunday at 19:34 Martin replied:

Not actually all my handiwork, surprisingly. I only wrote:
'The Jester was the least ridiculous person involved.' By the way,
are you not seeing Barney tonight?

On Sunday at 19:40 Ella replied:

About the play: I believe you. Good luck getting anyone else
to.
About Barney: I'm going to have to not see him tonight. In
fact, it's possible that that little business may have to be put on
hold. Something came up at Church this morning. Or rather,
someone.
Ella

On Sunday at 19:43 Martin replied:

Ella!
I will never lend you an idiot again. Stay the hell away from
Ross. Although the state of his bedroom should be sufficient
deterrent. I knew this would happen. I must admit I wouldn't
have predicted the exact circumstances. Church? I thought you
started sizzling if you crossed holy ground.

On Sunday at 19:55 Ella replied:

Alpha Course. It's the new supermarket, as far as pulling goes.
Should be an article in that somewhere. You should try it.
And I didn't break Barney - you did.

On Sunday at 20:05 Martin replied:

Don't follow.

On Sunday at 20:11 Ella replied:

He spent yesterday afternoon trying to mount his own
critique of Sartre's ontology. Not quite what I had planned for
us, you might say. Also, he kept insisting on leaping out of bed to
play me records. He really is crap at DJing, isn't he?

By the way, my comment was 'As a greengrocer I was
greatly misled by the title of this play. The evening featured no
vegetable's at all. I want my money back.'

Best Man

Hi Mike

Shame you couldn't make it to Chris and Emily's drinks on Friday. I hear you have been away on a corporate brainwashing weekend. Ah, the perks of the high-flying young professional. Have you heard the big news?

Martin

On Monday at 9:08 Mike replied:

Once again, you've got me bang to rights, Martin. The *training* weekend, as we here refer to it, involved an hour-long lecture and an all-expenses-paid weekend in a Scottish castle. Damn, damn, how I regret my life choices. Are they still making you clock out every time you go to the loo?

Of course I know about Chris and Emily. In fact I've known they've been planning it for months.

On Monday at 9:11 Martin replied:

I don't suppose Chris has mentioned anything about who he's asking to be his best man? I did ask but he hasn't got back to me, and I don't want to seem to be fishing...

On Monday at 9:18 Mike replied:

Actually, Martin, he has. Chris and Emily asked me to do it, a few weeks ago. I said I was sure you wouldn't be upset.

On Monday at 9:21 Martin replied:

Of course I'm not. I am a little bemused, though... Do you know if I made the short-list?

On Monday at 9:24 Mike replied:

Oh, Martin, I'm sure they would have asked you if, say, I was tragically schmoozed to death, Chris's brother disappeared, and Barney died in a freak DJing accident. I think what finally swung it for me was the brief presentation I gave Chris and Emily outlining my vision of what I would bring to the role. After a lot of blue-skying and spit-balling, I went for the simple yet powerful slogan: 'For your Best Man, choose the Best Man'. I used Powerpoint and everything.

Either that, or they simply went with the person they liked and trusted more. I admit it's hard to understand why they wouldn't want a bloke who can manage to lose his wallet and jacket in his own kitchen to be in charge of the rings.

By the way, how are things going with your housemate?

On Monday at 9:30 Martin replied:

Nice segue. I don't know why you think I'm so bothered about it. To be honest, it's a little bit sad that you're making so much of it. It's not like it literally means you're the best man. Or even a better man. Frankly, I wouldn't want all the hassle.

If you're genuinely interested, things with Ross are fine. He's hardly ever there, for one thing. We occasionally cross paths over breakfast or when he knocks on my door to tell me we need more loo-roll. Supposedly he's writing a sitcom, but I haven't seen much evidence of it. I think he's worried about me stealing his ideas, but as he's pitching it as a cross between *Coupling* and *No Logo* I think he can put his mind at rest on that front...

On Monday at 9:30 Mike replied:

Glad you're being so mature about the best man thing. Can't wait to see Ross's sitcom. Has he got a title? How about *Two Pints of Lager, Globalization and its Discontents, and a Packet of Crisps*?

In case you're wondering, Emily's already chosen her bridesmaids. Not that you wouldn't look lovely in a dress...

Re: Re: Review

Hey Martin,

Yes, I heard about the wedding and called to congratulate Chris and Emily. It should be a lovely day. Hope you're not too upset about not making best man. I have to confess I can sort of see their reasoning, though.

I presume the online comments about the play are yours? They will be coming down shortly and I would be grateful if you could restrain yourself. Not funny, just bitter.

Best wishes,

Sally

\-

On Monday at 11:02 Martin replied:

Look forward to seeing you at the wedding then.

I swear to God that the comments aren't mine. I'm sure you know me well enough to know that I'd have gone for something a bit more witty than 'That was no way a real horse.' And come on, the response to that was quite funny.

Martin

\-

On Monday at 11:12 Sally replied:

'Not the only person making a horse's ass of themselves onstage'? It's really sad that people have to snipe from the shadows this way.

\-

On Monday at 11:24 Martin replied:

Sniping from the shadows. If only I had thought of that…

On Monday at 11:27 Sally replied:

Pathetic. I hope you aren't going to be like this at the wedding. Seriously, stop it now.

On Monday at 11:35 Martin replied:

Actually, I was referring to the comment that 'The back end of the horse provided a useful clue as to the manner in which this play was created.' But I agree, it's sad and petty. And I assure you it's not me. Not all me, at any rate.

I think the personal attacks on David are unjustified and offensive. I would never stoop to demanding that someone 'stakes him through the heart and burns his corpse at a crossroads, to prevent a repetition of this crime against theatre.' Perhaps it's one of his exes who describes him as 'a loathsome animated voodoo doll' and adds 'I would stab him in the head with a pin, but I don't want to give Malcolm McLaren a headache!!!!' I'd never use that many exclamation marks. I find the whole thing distasteful, and your implication that I am either behind it or revelling in it offensive.

Martin

On Monday at 11:36 Martin wrote:

Hey Lucy

Check out the online reviews of David and Sally's play. The
public has shown its thumb, and it is pointing firmly downwards.
At last, something to restore my faith in the human spirit!!!!
Love
Martin

P.S. You haven't eloped, have you? REPLY TO ME

Ella

On Monday at 11:52 Barney wrote:

Did you know Ella was going to dump me? I'm absolutely gutted mate. God knows what I did wrong. Did she say anything to you?

On Monday at 11:57 Martin replied:

Of course not. All I heard was what a tiger you are. Women, eh? Ah well, God moves in mysterious ways, mate.

On Monday at 12:04 Barney replied:

Cheers, mate. Knew I could count on you.

Sally and David are pretty upset about the online reviews, by the way.

On Monday at 12:06 Martin replied:

It's not bloody me!

I think I could do a bit better than writing 'My arse ate my trousers it was so bored during this farrago.'

No one seems to be knocking you or Sally personally.

On Monday at 12:12 Barney replied:

You don't count 'Sally Kendle couldn't convey urgency of emotion if she was shouting "Fire!" in a burning orphanage' as personal?

On Monday at 12:15 Martin replied:

If you scroll down, someone has added 'And I wish she was.' But it really wasn't me.

Re: Neglected

Hi Martin,
Glad to see the family guilt-trip gene has survived another generation. Staying up here to try to earn a bit of cash for next term. Bloody bar-work. Thinking about applying to be part of one of those medical experiments they pay you cash for. If one more punter tells me to 'Cheer up, love, it may never happen,' I'm signing up. No matter if it's with Dr Frankenstein. Tempted to reply: 'It already has happened. I'm looking glum because I have to serve pints in this alleged funpub to people like you, i.e. the kind of twat who would spend time in this idiot sanctuary without having to be paid to do so.'
I wonder if they take requests for what experiment they do to you? I want a big ear on my back.
By the way, I've seen yourtheatre.com. Been busy? What have you got against Barney?
Lots of love,
Lucy

On Monday at 12:35 Martin wrote:

Nothing.

On Monday at 12:45 Lucy wrote:

I quote: 'I was prepared to salute the bravery and talent of DJ Idiot, but only because I had been misinformed that he has flippers instead of arms.'

On Monday at 13:04 Martin wrote:

That is sick. Possibly Ella.
I swear to God I only wrote one thing on there. Why will no one believe me?

On Monday at 13:07 Lucy wrote:

Because you have the motivation, and it fits your MO. Which is yours, then? The thing about the voodoo doll? Or is it the simple yet damning observation 'I now know I have 246 veins on the inside of my eyelids. I counted twice to check'?
By the way, sorry to hear about your public cuckolding. Bummer.

On Monday at 14:04 Martin replied:

Yeah, tell me about it. I guess Mum told you. Maybe she's behind the internet slander campaign.
I had lunch with Laura, who doesn't believe me about the online messages, either. Dammit, I think she's getting back together with her ex. Actually, come to think of it, when I spoke to Mum the other day, she was asking what Laura's surname was. Bit odd, surely?
On which note, I have been involved with a little internet jiggery-pokery. Let's just say that Acklington Stanley have acquired a new fan who is not all they appear...

On Monday at 14:48 Lucy replied:

Acklington Stanley. Who are they?

On Monday at 14:49 Martin replied:

Exactly.

On Monday at 14:56 Lucy replied:

Glad to hear you are channelling your energies to good effect. I have an inkling why Mum might be interested in Laura's surname, but I'll let you work it out for yourself.

Things going well with Sam.

On Monday at 14:57 Martin replied:

Only 'well'?

On Monday at 15:02 Lucy replied:

Yeah, you know, everything's perfect, and everyone thinks he's lovely, but there's something missing. It's probably me being overcritical and unable to accept happiness. I can't quite put my finger on what's odd there. He's charming, he's funny, he's fairly gorgeous.

On Monday at 15:04 Martin replied:

Has he only got one leg?

On Monday at 15:06 Lucy replied:

No, it's not that. What's Laura's surname?

On Monday at 15:08 Martin replied:

Don't laugh.

On Monday at 15:10 Lucy replied:

No, 'cos you were so understanding when I went out with Charlie Kerton.

On Monday at 15:12 Martin replied:

Charlie Curtain? Are you certain? Didja go steady or were ya just flirtin'? Got to stop - my sides are hurtin'.
Her surname is Mutton.

On Monday at 15:13 Lucy replied:

Oh dear, snorted tea onto my keyboard.
Well, she should be keen to get married.

On Monday at 15:15 Martin replied:

Actually, and bizarrely, she mentioned early on that she wants to keep her name. I should make it clear that we were speaking generally. So, in the unlikely event of our nuptials, she would be Mutton-Sargent.

On Monday at 15:17 Lucy replied:

Or Sargent-Mutton. Who sounds like someone who'd turn up in one of those hideous *Punch* cartoons about the Napoleonic Wars or the Crimea that you used to have to analyse in A-Level History.

On Monday at 15:19 Martin replied:

Man, were they ever funny! Dr Greaves used to crease up at those. Ho ho ho, look at Madame Thames dancing with King Cholera. Tee Hee, look at the Russian Bear being barked at by the British Bulldog. What was Turkey? Can't remember.
On which note, there is a deeply unfunny email entitled 'George's Bush' which I won't bother sending you.

On Monday at 15:21 Lucy replied:

Umm, surely Turkey was a Turkey?
Have seen 'George's Bush'. Mum sent it to me, of all people. She's getting quite web-happy these days.

On Monday at 15:22 Martin replied:

Or perhaps an Ottoman. Oh well, that's milked that one pretty dry.

On Monday at 15:23 Lucy replied:

I'm still laughing at Laura's surname.
Oh, oh, oh, by the way, Miriam is single. Frank dumped her! Right at the start of the holidays, too. You better move fast, though, she's having dinner with sinister Rupert tonight.

But perhaps you don't want fresh meat if you're lusting after mutton? Gotta go - meeting Sam. But what is it that's missing? It's going to really annoy me now.

Can't wait till you figure out why Mum needed to know Laura's surname. It's freaky ...

On Monday at 15:26 Martin replied:

What? What? What? Is there a family secret I don't know about? Do you know why the milkman whistles so gaily round our way?

Re: Re: Re: Review

On Monday at 15:34 Barney wrote:

Flippers, you bastard?

On Monday at 15:35 Martin replied:

Whatcha gonna do? Give me a slap?
IT WASN'T ME

The Mutton Mystery

On Monday at 15:45 Elizabeth Sargent wrote:

Hi, Martin,
So which Laura Mutton is she? The radical cheerleader, the one who breeds Wiemeranas, the one who does watercolours of Stevie Nicks, or the one at goocoveredgirls.com? Don't think I should investigate too closely into the last one.
Lots of love,

Mum

On Monday at 15:46 Martin replied:

MUM! Are you googling people I fancy?

On Monday at 15:56 Elizabeth Sargent replied:

Well, I like to know what's going on. You should try it with Lucy's new boy. I wonder if he's the Sam Bonar who was arrested in Mexico for practising medicine without a licence? Or the Fire Chief of Paradise City, New Jersey? Probably not. He did go on the uni ski trip two years ago - there's a picture. But he has a ski mask on. Still, it's amazing what you can uncover.

On Monday at 15:57 Martin replied:

Hold up. Sam's surname is Bonar? Strangely Lucy neglected to mention that. Very interesting...

I'll check with Laura about her 'hobbies'.

On Monday at 16:00 Elizabeth Sargent replied:

Don't you dare. By the way, I know it's Mummish and you'll
roll your eyes, but I've sent you a brochure for an Alpha course.
They're very popular nowadays, you know. You can meet all
sorts of people you wouldn't expect at that kind of thing. So
maybe give it a try.

And by the way I looked at yourtheatre.com when I was
online. I don't think some of those are in very good taste, Martin.
I do worry about where some of this stuff comes from ...

On Monday at 16:03 Martin replied:

So you google my exes, too? It wasn't bloody me! God, what
do people take me for?

As regards Alpha, it might surprise you to know that I've
been hearing good things about it myself. I have heard you meet
all sorts there. May check it out. Thanks for thinking of me.
This doesn't mean I've forgiven you for that Easter camp. Every
bloody day singing 'Jesus, Prince of Thieves' and wandering
around in the woods.

On Monday at 16:08 Elizabeth Sargent wrote:

I don't know where you get this guilt-tripping streak from.
You'll never let me forget that, will you? I thought it would be
fun. And as you well know, it's 'Jesus, Prince of Peace'.

On Monday at 16:09 Martin replied:

Not the way we sang it. And whoever catered that hellpit will

179

need to turn the other cheek a fair few times if I ever meet them. There were three hundred hungry teens who would have killed for five loaves and three fishes...

Rainbow Club, my arse.

On Monday at 16:11 Elizabeth Sargent replied:

I think you made your point at the time. I do remember the embarrassment of having to pick up the child who instituted a chant of 'We want Barabbas!' during the closing festivities. One of the counsellors suggested we consider having you exorcised. At the time, we thought it was a silly idea ...

On Monday at 16:13 Martin wrote:

Hi Laura
This may sound like a bit of an odd question, but my mum was wondering if that's you on goocoveredgirls.com? It's kind of hard to tell with all that stuff on your face. Only way to check I suppose is to discover whether you have a flaming skull tattooed on your hip.

On Monday at 16:14 Laura replied:

You're far from the first to ask me that. No, it's not me. Bit odd of your mum to ask, but not as unsettling as when my gran wanted to know. Ewww. I'm not that freaky Stevie Nicks fan, either. I expect another warning from the internet-misuse monitors is winging its way to you as we speak, sicko.

180

Sam

On Monday at 20:19 Lucy wrote:

I figured out what it is about Sam!

On Tuesday at 9:01 Martin replied:

Is it his surname?

On Tuesday at 9:03 Lucy replied:

I take it you spoke to Mum. No, it's not that. I realised as we were sitting there having dinner, he's really boring. He looks nice, and he talks about quite interesting things, and his voice isn't too bad, but everything he says is ... Readybrek. And then you find yourself being boring, too, because you haven't been paying attention. And then the candles start going in and out of focus. I have forkmarks in my thigh from stabbing myself to stay awake.
Bollocks.

On Tuesday at 9:04 Martin replied:

Surely it's good that you figured it out. Now you can break up and move on.

On Tuesday at 9:05 Lucy replied:

Well, what am I going to tell him?

On Tuesday at 9:06 Martin replied:

Why not say: 'You sap my will to live with your mysterious ability to churn dross out of conversational gold, but don't worry there are probably lots of girls who will like it.'

On Tuesday at 9:07 Lucy replied:

No, the rule is you only tell someone things like that if they can change it. Like if they have a hairy back.

On Tuesday at 9:08 Martin replied:

Or a crap surname.

On Tuesday at 9:10 Lucy replied:

Indeed. I tried to tell him this morning.

On Tuesday at 9:12 Martin replied:

This morning?!?

On Tuesday at 9:14 Lucy replied:

I told you, he's only boring when he talks ... Gotta go, he's bringing breakfast in.
Oh, by the way, *is* that Laura on goocoveredgirls.com? Gross ... Nice tattoo, though.

Re: Sam

On Tuesday at 14:12 Lucy wrote:

Oops! Sam saw the forkprints on my leg.

On Tuesday at 14:15 Martin replied:

Wow, I thought that was a figure of speech.
So you explained and now you're free/alone (delete according to taste)?

On Tuesday at 14:16 Lucy replied:

Not exactly. He asked me if I was self-harming. He did a course on it and everything. Apparently he had a girlfriend before who did that.

On Tuesday at 14:17 Martin replied:

Did you suggest that he might have driven her to it with his … zzzz. Sorry, drifted off.

On Tuesday at 14:19 Lucy replied:

The same wicked thought crossed my mind, too. But he was really noble and sweet about it. I made up an excuse, but I don't think he bought it. He put some leaflets in my pigeon-hole earlier.

On Tuesday at 14:21 Martin replied:

I take it that's not an unusually unpleasant double entendre. What was your excuse?

\-

On Tuesday at 14:23 Lucy replied:

Er, I said a cat did it.

\-

On Tuesday at 14:25 Martin replied:

Presumably a cat hopping up and down your thigh on one foot?
That's so absurd. So now he's obviously convinced that you actually are self-harming?

\-

On Tuesday at 14:26 Lucy replied:

Yeah. He was asking all about our family and my childhood. He was being so sweet.

\-

On Tuesday at 14:28 Martin replied:

Oh God. What did you tell him?

\-

On Tuesday at 14:34 Lucy replied:

I may have mentioned the French Service Station Incident. And about the Hide and Seek prank. He looked very serious. I think he was a bit puzzled by the 'Bombardiez' gag.
Anyway, I really upset him by telling him I wasn't going to ask for help. But now I can't break up with him, you see.

\-

On Tuesday at 14:38 Martin replied:

Don't see at all. Sounds like the perfect excuse. He must be desperate to get away from you. No offence.

On Tuesday at 14:45 Lucy replied:

Weirdly, exactly the opposite. Now we have something to talk about, and he's all excited and protective. And if I break up with him now he'll think it's because he discovered my dark secret and be all worried. He just slipped a card from the Union shop with a smiley lion on it under my door.

On Tuesday at 14:47 Martin replied:

Smiley lion? Dump him. Dump him now.

P.S. Christ, if my kids were going to have the surname Sargent-Bonar, I wouldn't be messing about.

Re: Ross

On Tuesday at 15:03 Mike wrote:

All right, mate,

Still bitter about not being best man? I've had a thought about that. How about if I ask Chris if we could give you an honorary title of some kind? Something like 'Understudy to the Best Man' or 'Assistant Best Man'? Maybe 'Second-Best Man'?

Actually, that's not the chief reason I'm emailing. In fact, I've made a bit of a strange discovery.

Mike

On Tuesday at 15:15 Martin replied:

If this is about goocoveredgirls.com, I know. My mum told me.

On Tuesday at 15:17 Mike replied:

Well, that's one way of explaining about the birds and the bees, I guess. Nothing like breaking it to you gently, is there?

No, seriously, this is properly odd.

On Tuesday at 15:18 Martin replied:

Your financial backstabbing and desperate corporate ladder climbing has left you spiritually empty and paranoid as to who your real friends are? Or if you have any? There are some spiritual vacuums not even paintballing and fantasising about my sister can fill? I have a book that might help - I believe the void you are feeling inside may well be Jesus-shaped, my friend. I hear good things about the Alpha course...

On Tuesday at 15:22 Mike replied:

No, no, not that. Although of course that's true. God, it's unfulfilling being a soulless suit. Why do I do it? Oh yes, money, respect, power, and, most of all, not to be a temp loser like you.

On Tuesday at 15:25 Martin replied:

Actually, I got taken on here permanently last November, so up yours, Gordon Gekko.

On Tuesday at 15:32 Mike replied:

Martin, Martin, Martin. Now *that* was the response of a sad and broken man. Join me, Martin, join me ... you'll like it as one of us ... we're a big happy family ...

On Tuesday at 15:35 Martin replied:

I'd rather die than join the Dark Side.

On Tuesday at 15:40 Mike replied:

Cute, but actually, the entrance procedure here is highly competitive, and you're not really cut from the kind of officer material we're looking for, if you know what I mean. But one of our tea-ladies is off sick.
Do you want to know what I found out or not?

On Tuesday at 15:45 Martin replied:

You're gay?
We all knew that, Mike.

On Tuesday at 15:48 Mike replied:

Martin,
My time is valuable, even if yours is not. I know where your
flatmate goes at all hours, and he isn't sitting writing in some
café in North Brent and hoping no one throws him out or nicks
his laptop.

On Tuesday at 16:12 Martin replied:

I don't live in North Brent. It's easy to distinguish: North
Brent is where they do the shooting. Kensal Green is in South
Brent, where they dump the bodies.

On Tuesday at 16:15 Mike replied:

Whatever. The point is I met your boy today. I went for a
big corporate lunch with people from another firm, and he was
there.

On Tuesday at 16:17 Martin replied:

So:
Ross works in Spearmint Rhino?
Ross hands out breathmints in the toilets at a restaurant?

On Tuesday at 16:36 Mike replied:

Your flatmate works for Grimble, Mallet and Spoke. He ain't writing no sitcom.

On Tuesday at 16:38 Martin replied:

I don't follow. What is that?

On Tuesday at 16:45 Mike replied:

Pretty hot consultancy firm. Ross has a fully fledged secret identity - as a management consultant.

On Tuesday at 16:52 Martin replied:

Well, fuck me. I knew that samurai sword was a bad sign.

On Tuesday at 16:57 Mike replied:

By the way, I think you might have gone a bit far with those comments on yourtheatre.com. Some of them made me chuckle, though.

On Tuesday at 16:58 Martin replied:

OH FOR THE LAST TIME IT'S NOT ME.
Anyway, about time for me to be getting home. Only about five more hours for you, eh?

On Tuesday at 17:02 Mike replied:

Nah, Tuesday night our Dark Master cashes up early, 'cos he likes to get back for the redecorating programmes on BBC2. I'm about to start helping him load the sacks full of souls into the little train in the basement.

Re: Re: Sam

Crap. Was making tea on the shitty little fucking kettle in my room and managed to scald my wrist. Another typical piece of Sargent-family crapware. Like those bloody calculators.

On Wednesday at 9:04 Martin replied:

Yeah. I could have been Carol Vorderman by now if I hadn't gone through school with a calculator Dad got as a freebie from a Dental Floss company. Cosines? Tangents? Forget it. You had to turn it upside down and press 'multiply' to get it to divide.

But was it really an accident?

On Wednesday at 9:19 Lucy replied:

Don't you start. I had Sam on at me half the night. Although he did reveal that 'Chubby Chris' went through a similar 'phase' at school. Quelle surprise. Sam confirmed that she also had an army surplus bag but couldn't think of anything to write on it. Perhaps 'Pies. Hands Off. For future regurgitation' would have been appropriate. I suggested that if I was Christine I'd be tempted to self-harm as well, but Sam didn't think that was anything to joke about. Did you know that the hardest thing about fighting teenage self-harm is changing attitudes and getting people to take it seriously? Oh my God I'm dating the *Guardian*.

Did you know we use humour as a defence mechanism in our family?

On Wednesday at 9:24 Martin replied:

He's right. Use it as a defence mechanism against him.

P.S. Jokes about Teen Depression are Nut jokes.

On Wednesday at 9:28 Lucy replied:

I'm afraid I accidentally used his smiley lion as an ashtray, too.

On Wednesday at 9:34 Martin replied:

No such thing as an accident. You did it because you are angry and hostile towards yourself and are striking out at him.

On Wednesday at 9:38 Lucy replied:

Uncanny. How did you know? Presumably I am projecting my own inner blankness onto him as well, but I didn't say anything about that. Oh, I didn't mention it before because I knew what your response would be, but he has a beard.

On Wednesday at 9:43 Martin replied:

He's a Jesus-shaped arsehole!

On Wednesday at 9:44 Lucy replied:

He thinks you may have anger issues that you refuse to confront.

On Wednesday at 10:12 Martin replied:

Brilliant diagnosis, Dr Bonar. Come here and say that to my face and I'll show you anger issues with a fucking mallet.

On Wednesday at 10:14 Lucy replied:

Well, he may have a point ...

On Wednesday at 10:20 Martin replied:

What is he? A first-year psychology student?

On Wednesday at 10:21 Lucy replied:

Third-year geographer.

On Wednesday at 10:22 Martin replied:

Jesus, if that's not a bloody great warning I don't know what it. But if he's analysing our family, who's colouring in the map and counting the pebbles?
There's no other option. Do the beard gag on him.

On Wednesday at 10:26 Lucy replied:

I'm saving it for when I really need it. You don't do the beard gag unless you mean it. There's no going back from the beard gag.

Pretty in Pink

On Wednesday at 10:35 Martin wrote:

Hey Ella
Any truth in the rumour that Emily's asked you to be a
bridesmaid? This I can't wait to see…

On Wednesday at 10:40 Ella replied:

Don't even start to go there, Sargent. I won't begin to number
the ways in which this goes against the grain with me. I'm
starting to suspect the whole wedding thing is an elaborate ploy
to see me dolled up in pink.

On Wednesday at 10:42 Martin replied:

It does baffle the imagination. I more pictured you appearing
at their first christening with a cackle and a puff of smoke. No
offence.

On Wednesday at 10:45 Ella replied:

Sure. After all, why would I be offended at being compared to
a bitter old witch? To make matters worse, the other bridesmaids
are Emily's teenage cousins. I don't know whether we're having
a hen-night or a sleepover. On the positive side, though, this is
exactly how I planned on bumping into Barney again.

On Wednesday at 10:47 Martin replied:

Really? How so?

On Wednesday at 10:51 Ella replied:

Firstly, I don't want to see Barney, full stop. Secondly, if I do have to see him, I seldom look my best done up like Little Bo Peep, taking part in a patriarchal ceremony about which I am at best ambivalent, and surrounded by a bunch of fresh-faced nubiles.

And if you see Mike, tell him if he thinks he can try it on with me because he's best man, he's messing with the wrong fucking bridesmaid.

Acklington Stanley

On Wednesday at 11:05 Laura wrote:

Hello, all,
Writing to let you know that the Wednesday after next my
boyfriend's new band, Acklington Stanley, will be playing
in Camden (flyer attached). The new songs are really good.
Some of them are about me! I think any of you who remember
Fork would be advised to remain open-minded (open-eared?).
Anyway, the flyer is pretty self-explanatory. The beer is cheap,
and the glasses plastic. Indie disco after for those who don't care
it's midweek and the floor is sticky.
Lots of love,

Laura

UPSTAIRS AT THE CAMDEN TAVERN
'KEEPING MUSIC LIVE SINCE 1985'

19 OLD GLUE FACTORY LANE.
CAMDEN TOWN TUBE

WEDNESDAY JULY 6

acklington stanley

FEAT. FORMER JAZZBUCKET DRUMMER
JEZ MOORE

SUPPORT FROM

The Lost Cause

Bar from 8. Support Act at 8:30.
£6/£4.50 Students
Disco until 12 (60s/70s/80s/Alternative)
The Camden Tavern operates a zero-tolerance
policy on drugs
R.O.A.R.

On Wednesday at 11:06 Martin wrote:

Hi Laura

I don't have anyone to point out the absurdities of this flyer to except you. I see there is support from The Lost Cause. Please God tell me they are a slightly obscurely-named tribute band. Lovely-looking girls, shame about Jim.

Could you not suggest to your boyfriend that the name Acklington Stanley is perhaps an in-joke too far? I mean, the Rolling Stones took their name from a Muddy Waters tune; Led Zeppelin was originally a joke of Keith Moon's; Steely Dan is the name of a dildo. But a reference to an 80s Milk Marketing Board promotion? If I had to pick one thing and put it in a time capsule to explain the 'spirit' of indie, that name would be it. They must be kicking themselves about John Peel...

Hold on. Gwyn is your boyfriend again?

Martin

On Wednesday at 11:12 Laura replied:

Yes, it all sort of happened over the weekend. I had been meaning to tell you. Hope you're not upset.

On Wednesday at 11:13 Martin replied:

Upset? No, why would I be? See you around, and probably at the gig.

Re: Re: Fork Is Genius!

On Wednesday at 18:01 Johannes Jester wrote:

Dear darling Gwyn

I am hearing you have a new band. I am excited about the
Acklington Stanley and hope they play at my home town real
soon. It is such a good name - strong, mysterious, evocative.
Exactly like your music. One day when my mother dies I would
love to visit the hamlet of Camden. Perhaps you could show me
around.

But I worry does this mean no more Forkmusic? Please don't
say it's true!!!???!!!

Love

Johannes

On Wednesday at 19:35 Gwyn replied:

Hey Johanna,

You heard right. From the ashes of Fork has risen...
Acklington Stanley. Well, to be fair, we have all of us been in
bands before. Our bass player Johnno was in the Mucky Faces;
our drummer Jez was in Herbalessence (known in certain
territories as JazzBucket for legal reasons); Mark, our lead guitar,
was in Overpass and The Kids. So you can imagine there's a
lot of excitement about us all playing together! The *Camden
Flyer* has already labelled us a 'supergroup', but that's not really
the angle we want to play up. Hopefully people will leave their
preconceptions at the door, and judge us on our music. People
are ready for something new after all the artificial Crap Idol stuff
of the last few years. And Acklington Stanley is it!

I would love to show you around Camden, I hope your mother dies soon. Only kidding!!!

Lotsa love

Gwyn

P.S. It's amazing that we can keep in touch with all our fans through the internet these days. I'm thinking of you reading this all the way in Germany. What are you wearing? Grrrowl.

On Wednesday at 19:48 Johannes Jester replied:

Dear Gwyn

I am wearing solely my pink housecleaning coat and a pointy helmet. What are you wearing?

But does this mean there is no more Fork? Everyone in Dusseldorf will be weeping and wailing. There may be a 'Sad Riot' (to quote one of your song-titles!). I don't believe it.

I am a little upset with you.

Love

Johannes

On Wednesday at 20:15 Gwyn replied:

Dear Johanna,

Sounds pretty sexy! Are you serious? I'm wearing skinny drainpipes and a pair of aviators. I was wearing a vest, but I took it off...

What are you doing now?

Gwyn

On Wednesday at 20:23 Johannes wrote:

Dear Gwyn

I am tearing down all my posters of Fork and screwing them

up in balls and jumping on them. I am SO ANGRY!!! I hope
Acklington Stanley are the big flop and you have to reform
Fork right away. My mother is angry too and she says it is
DISGUSTING how you treat your fans. You are sell-out and
traitor. Even thought of you with no vest is not pleasant to me at
this time.

Love
Johannes

P.S. Put your vest back on. Johannes is a bloke's name,
dickhead.

Part Six

The Worst Play in the World

Milk • Bread • Mr Socky
Issues • The Intervention
The Book • The Old Barney Magic
Names

Milk

Long time no see, flatmate

Listen, I used the last of the milk this morning. I was
wondering if you could pick some up on the way home? Are
you going to be around tonight? I can't remember the last
time we SPOKE. Also I don't want to GRIMBLE, but could
we CONSULT about dividing up the bills sometime? Hope the
'sitcom' is going well.

Martin

On Monday at 14:35 Ross replied:

Oh God. Who told you? Don't suppose you would believe that
I have an evil twin? I swear I really am planning on writing this
sitcom, though.

The Big Questions

On Monday at 15:12 Ella wrote:

Hi, Martin,
I think we need to stage an intervention between Sally and David.
Ella

On Monday at 15:15 Martin replied:

Intervention? I don't follow.

On Monday at 15:18 Ella replied:

I had dinner with them last night. I ran out of excuses not to. He's truly appalling. We need to break them up. I know that sounds cruel but it's for the best.
Ella

On Monday at 15:25 Martin replied:

Ella, I've been saying this for weeks. But why is it all of a sudden for the best? Is Sally unhappy?

On Monday at 15:34 Ella replied:

Sally is completely radiant and bubbly as ever. Boy, you guys really weren't suited, were you? I don't think I've ever seen her this happy. It's not for the benefit of David or Sally, it's for my sake. Another dinner like that and I will lose the will to live.

So! You! Make! Bread! Enough already. 'I love to get my hands doughy, it really puts me in touch with what matters in life'. What? Yeast? Stop the search for the meaning of life everyone, it's in David's kitchen.

And that fucking bread tastes horrible. I nearly chipped a tooth.

No, it's abhorrent how happy they are together. It's all little pecks on the cheek when they think you're not looking. Sally ended up perching on his lap at the end of the evening. They were talking about the future. Like, kids. Like, moving out of London.

On Monday at 15:42 Martin replied:

NO! Well, it does happen, Ella. You know we're all getting to the age when we start thinking about growing up.

It's astonishing I ever open an email from you. Every one is like a hammer blow to the back of the head. I'm glad Sally is happy. I may not be the best person to intervene. We're not really in communication.

On Monday at 15:48 Ella replied:

I'm just trying to stir you into action. By the way, I didn't know you rang Sally up drunk...

On Monday at 16:05 Martin replied:

Yeah, not one of my prouder moments. From a period in my life which isn't exactly throwing up an abundance of them. I mounted a fairly detailed and sustained critique of David then, if I recall correctly, and it didn't get me anywhere.

On Monday at 16:15 Ella replied:

You really are a class act, aren't you? I quote: 'I must still like you, I sat through your shitty play.' 'I'm writing a novel about our relationship.' 'What's it called?' 'I'm thinking of entitling it *I Hate David, and He Smells of Floorboards.*' Oh I almost forgot the piece de la resistance: 'I have to go now. I'm still really angry and I have loads to say, but the room is spinning and I think I'm going to be sick.' Nice work, Cyrano.

On Tuesday at 9:04 Martin replied:

Yes, well there's more than one way to say I love you. I take it she wasn't won back?

On Tuesday at 10:21 Ella replied:

I think not. Baffled, yes. Upset, yes. But not won back. Apparently at one point you put a sock on your hand?

On Tuesday at 10:25 Martin replied:

Yes, I thought I might have done that.

On Tuesday at 10:30 Ella replied:

Pretty pointless over the phone I should have thought.

On Tuesday at 10:34 Martin replied:

It used to be one of our games when we were upset with each other. You know: 'Mrs Socky says she felt you were a bit selfish about Sally's mother coming to stay', 'Mr Socky says have a good time when you're out with the girls and he has to stay home with boring Martin.'

On Tuesday at 10:37 Ella replied:

That is truly sick.

PS Why floorboards, if you don't mind me asking?

On Tuesday at 10:40 Martin replied:

I didn't say I was proud of it. Anyway, Mr Socky let Sally know how he felt about how she treated Martin.

P.S. Because I don't ever get close enough to floorboards to smell them, and I don't ever want to get close enough to David to smell him. It seemed a very obvious connection at the time.
P.P.S. Mr Socky tells me that he is willing to help with the 'intervention'. But what in particular has triggered all this off? I mean, we have agreed in the past that we both think he's a bit of a twat. What's new?

On Tuesday at 10:43 Ella replied:

It struck me when David was talking about his new play. He actually called Sally his 'muse' at one point. And I had a vision that if we don't stop him now it may be too late. And you won't be able to read the paper or listen to the radio or watch the TV without him opining and pontificating. It was around the point when he said 'Today the New Place, tomorrow the world.' And I realised he might very well do it. But to be honest, now I know about Mr and Mrs Socky I'm beginning to think Sally might be better off staying put with him.

PS Are you really writing a novel called *I Hate David, and He Smells of Floorboards*? I'd love to read it.

On Tuesday at 10:48 Martin replied:

No, I'm not. I've given up writing novels about people I know. And I haven't written anything at all since Sally left.

P.S. She's not my muse. She just took all the pens.
P.P.S. So what is David's new play about?

On Tuesday at 11:01 Ella replied:

This is it. I realised as he was talking about the play that somewhere in our society the idiot filter is broken, and there's nothing to stop David unless we do it ourselves.

The new play, as you will recall from the *Chalk Farm Gazette*, is the one where he deals with issues of race, class, gender, sexuality and religion. And love. And war. And history. In 90 minutes.

On Tuesday at 11:06 Martin replied:

Is Sally in it?

On Tuesday at 11:11 Ella replied:

Oh yeah. So he was telling us about it, and believe me my fingers wince and my nails leak blood as I force myself to type this:

Sally is a backpacker in India who falls in love.

210

On Tuesday at 11:12 Martin replied:

OK. It sounds bad. In fact, it sounds terrible. I trust she falls in love against a background of conflict in a beautiful place...

On Tuesday at 11:15 Ella replied:

She does indeed. Guess what she has in her backpack?

On Tuesday at 11:17 Martin replied:

Imodium? *Rough Guide*? Beedis? Toilet roll?

On Tuesday at 11:21 Ella replied:

Letters her grandmother wrote ...

On Tuesday at 11:25 Martin replied:

... to the maharajah she had a fling with two generations before?
Damn. Now I need to think of a new idea for my next novel. Farewell, Man Booker Prize...

On Tuesday at 11:27 Ella replied:

Now, I know there are a million sound political reasons to object to this kind of pandering exoticising patronising crap. But more to the point: We Are Going to Have to Sit Through It.

On Tuesday at 11:29 Martin replied:

Nah, only you. I've got a sharp pencil and I'm about to pierce my eardrums and put my eyes out.

On Tuesday at 11:34 Ella replied:

Wait until you've read this, and then sharpen one for me too.
Me: So you must know a lot about the political and historical background?
David: I think coming to these things fresh is often an advantage.
Sally: I think we're going over together for a few weeks to soak up the atmosphere.
David: I always think what's most important is not that theatre provides answers, but that theatre asks the questions.
Me: I need a pee.

On Tuesday at 11:37 Martin replied:

Pencil poised. The questions being?

On Tuesday at 11:43 Ella replied:

I dunno. Is love good? Is war bad? Is racism bad? Do the deeds of history echo in the present?

On Tuesday at 11:52 Martin replied:

Oh good, I think I know the answers already. Does that mean I don't have to go/destroy eyesight and hearing? Off to do some research of my own.

On Tuesday at 12:00 Ella replied:

In what way?

On Tuesday at 12:02 Martin replied:

I've got floorboards to sniff.

By the way, I don't think an intervention will be necessary. The magic of being with David travelling around India for a few weeks should do the trick.

Re: Ella

On Tuesday at 13:09 Barney wrote:

Mate,
Listen, I need a straight answer. Ella isn't returning my calls or emails. Have you heard from her? I dunno what went wrong. Do you think there's any chance of getting back with her?
Depressed,
Best,
Barney

PS don't suppose Chris got back to you about me DJing at the wedding?

On Tuesday at 14:10 Martin wrote:

Hi Ella
Barney wants to know if you would ever consider getting back with him? What should I say? Any chance?
Martin

On Tuesday at 14:14 Ella replied:

Yeah. I ignore his calls and emails 'cos I'm desperate to rekindle that magic. What do you think?
I have explained this to him. Maybe I should have used shorter words. We. Were. A. Fling. When. I. Think. About. It. I. Feel. No. Nostalgia. Only. Vague. Nausea.
I suppose there is a minuscule chance things could get

rekindled. But there's a similar probability of Atlantis rising off the Isle of Wight, David Icke turning out to be the Messiah, and the new Oasis album genuinely being 'a massive return to form'.

Send him my regards.

Ella

On Tuesday at 14:17 Martin wrote:

Hi Barney

There is a slim possibility of your getting back together. VERY slim.

Martin

On Tuesday at 14:18 Barney replied:

What should I do?

On Tuesday at 14:20 Martin replied:

I'll ask. But if I were you, I'd give up on it. Seriously.

On Tuesday at 14:23 Martin wrote:

Hi Ella

What should Barney do?

Martin

On Tuesday at 14:34 Ella replied:

He should practise DJing. A lot.

On Tuesday at 14:35 Martin replied:

I'll suggest that. Let me rephrase: under what circumstances would you give Barney another try? What could he do to make that a more realistic possibility? I think he's saying he can change...

On Tuesday at 14:40 Ella replied:

Well, I have thought about this quite seriously over the past five minutes. It's sweet of him to offer to change. In a burst of over-generous reciprocity I've come up with a short list of things that he might think about changing.

Barney might possibly become attractive to me again if all the following criteria were fulfilled:
1 He had different hair
2 He had a different face
3 He had a different body
4 His voice was different
5 He behaved differently
6 He had a different name
7 He was a different person
8 He won the lottery
9 I was drunk
   But probably not even then.

On Tuesday at 14:45 Martin wrote:

Barney, I think it may be time to let this one go.

On Tuesday at 14:52 Barney replied:

It's because she thinks I'm thick, isn't it?

On Tuesday at 14:54 Martin replied:

Actually, that wasn't something she mentioned.

On Tuesday at 14:57 Ella wrote:

Oh yeah, and he would have to be a lot less thick.

On Tuesday at 15:03 Barney wrote:

Cheers for your advice, mate.

I guess there's not much hope. Let me know if she says anything about me. Well, let her know that there's always someone who'll be lapping up the old Barney magic.

Startin' again, Martin my friend
Barney

On Tuesday at 15:04 Martin wrote:

Bafflingly, that does indeed seem to be the case. Oh, there was one thing she did mention.

On Tuesday at 15:05 Barney wrote:

What was that?

On Tuesday at 15:07 Martin wrote:

Stop doing those godawful rhymed sign-offs. Honestly. Stop it. Now.

Barney

On Tuesday at 15:13 Martin wrote:

Hi Chris

Hope the wedding preparations are all in hand and Emily's
bulge isn't showing yet. Mate, have you given any thought
to letting Barney DJ for a bit? I know he ain't the best DJ in
the world, and may well be among the worst, but he'd really
appreciate it. He's not in a very good way at the mo about Ella
and I think it would help take his mind off things.
Love to Emily
Martin

On Wednesday at 12:14 Chris wrote:

Hi Martin,
Actually, I have been thinking about it. The other day Emily
and I were sitting around and she turned to me and said, 'Do you
know what would make our special day that extra-bit special,
Chris?'
And I said, 'What, my precious?'
And she said, 'I want us to have the worst DJ we can possibly
find.' And I thought of Barney, because the last time I saw him
play he managed to slice his thumb open on a 12" record. And he
was no worse with one hand than he is with two.
But then Emily and I realised we already know lots of people
who DJ. All of whom want to play at the wedding. Some of them
are quite good. All of them are better than Barney. My granny is
a better DJ than Barney. And she won't be DJing at the wedding,
either. Because she's dead.

But we had to find some way of choosing a DJ. So Emily said, 'You know, my little fruitplum, what would make our extra-special day even more extra-special than a crap DJ?'

And I said, 'No, my little rosebud, what could that be?'

And Emily said, 'A DJ who's not only crap, but who once described himself to you as an "art-noise-terrorist, messing with people's heads".'

And I said, 'Why, I know the very man you mean.'

But still there was something not quite right. I could see Emily was thinking about something. So I said, 'What is it, shnoozles? What furrows your little brow?'

And Emily said, 'You'll think I'm being silly. But I always wanted a DJ at my wedding who was really depressed and upset with women.'

And I said, 'That's amazing, pookie. It's what I've always dreamed of, too. But where can we possibly find one at such short notice?'

So you see, your email caught me at the perfect time.

Chris

On Wednesday at 12:16 Martin replied:

I take it you're being sarcastic. Couldn't you let him play in the corner, and unplug the speakers? I don't think he'd notice.

On Wednesday at 12:30 Chris replied:

Let me put it plainly. The only possible way we are going to let Barney spin a platter at our wedding is if he is dressed as a waiter and he is revolving a large round silver tray to offer someone a vol-au-vent.

On Wednesday at 12:34 Martin replied:

I'll tell him you already have someone booked.

On Wednesday at 12:40 Chris replied:

You do that.
Also, I think the best man is going to be in touch to ask about suggestions for the stag night. DO NOT suggest anything involving Finnish clowns, avant-garde origami or open-mike poetry. Or, indeed, Barney DJing.

Hi

On Thursday at 9:16 Martin wrote:

Hi Sally

Wondering how you are doing. I was thinking last night and I realise I may have taken this break-up thing badly. Really badly. I hope you know how much I treasure our time together, and how much you still mean to me. I think you are a truly amazing person, and I am so proud to see your talent receiving the recognition it deserves. (I don't mean the nasty comments on the website, I mean the good notices). Ella was telling me about the new play and it sounds intriguing. Best of luck with it. I guess when there's a breakup it's pointless to try and apportion the blame. We were something that wasn't meant to be, and the best we can do is to look on it as a learning experience, and both try to grow as people. Like flowers, if you will, out of the manure of our messy past. I have discussed it with Mr Socky and he agrees. I look forward to seeing you at the wedding.

Sincerely

Martin

On Thursday at 10:20 Sally replied:

Dear Martin,

I was moved by your sweet email. That's how I feel, too. It is silly, after all we've been through, to be on bad terms. I do have a lot of happy memories from our time together, and I'm sorry about how it ended. See you at the wedding.

Mrs Socky sends her regards also!

Affectionately,

Sally

On Thursday at 10:28 Martin replied:

Dear Sally
That's great. Now that we're friends again, can I make a
friendly suggestion?
Affectionately
Martin

On Thursday at 10:45 Sally replied:

Of course. But it isn't that creepy thing again about wearing
each other's clothes, is it? That wasn't appropriate then and it
certainly isn't appropriate now.
Sally

On Thursday at 11:22 Martin replied:

Of course not. Jesus, I was joking. You never let it lie, do you?
No this is something different.

On Thursday at 11:27 Sally replied:

Joking is when you suggest something once, Martin ...
On a similar note, I've already told you quite definitely that
I'm never going to change my name to 'Busty de Winter'. Even if
it would 'get the punters in'.
So what is this great suggestion?

On Thursday at 11:45 Martin replied:

I say this not as an ex, not because I am jealous, and not
because I hold any hope or even desire to get back together. As a
friend:

222

Dump the creep. Dump him, dump him, dump him.

Take him to the dump like a sofa that doesn't meet fire safety regulations.

Make like Stig, and Dump him.

Next time you have a dump, flush David.

Lots of Love

Martin

P.S. Mr Socky agrees. In fact, he feels even more strongly on the issue than I do.

On Thursday at 12:45 Sally replied:

Twat.

On Thursday at 13:14 Martin wrote:

At least say you'll consider the idea? Glad we're friends again.

Lots of Love

Martin

Congratulations

On Friday at 14:02 Ella wrote:

Good going, Martin. That was exactly what I had in mind.
Ella

On Friday at 14:10 Martin replied:

What? It was worth a try, surely?

On Friday at 14:45 Ella replied:

Twat.
By the way, glad you and Sally have decided to be mates. She
says never to contact her again.

On Friday at 15:02 Martin replied:

She is quite definite about that?

On Friday at 15:15 Ella replied:

I'd certainly give it a few weeks. But she's pretty nice, so
eventually she will no doubt forgive you.
    Christ, if you pulled this kind of crap with me you would be
in so much pain. And I don't mean 'Oh, my heart aches'. I mean
'Please, I can't bear to wait for the ambulance. Shoot me. Death
would be a release.'

Christ, you never think about what you're doing, do you?

On Friday at 15:17 Martin replied:

Oh Ella
I would prefer to be shot before I got involved with you, if it's all the same. Barney sends his love. Again.
Yes, I never think, do I?
I can't see Sally.
I can't talk to Sally.
I can't email Sally.
I'm not welcome at Sally's plays...
Man, I'm good.

On Friday at 15:19 Ella replied:

Dammit. You're a genius. A sick, twisted, bitter kind of genius, but a genius nevertheless.

On Friday at 15:46 Ella wrote:

Hi, Sally
I don't like David, either. He really does smell of floorboards. Damp floorboards with bodies under them in a house with bad feng shui. I abhor him. I don't think I could stand to be in the same room with him. Even if it is a large room with lots of chairs in it. Sorry. See you in a few months.
Lots of love, Ella

On Friday at 16:22 Sally wrote:

Dear Martin and Ella,
You guys are so lame. I expect to see you both at opening

night, where you can both grovel and try to make it up to me. And David.

Jesus, I had to read Martin's book …

On Friday at 16:30 Ella wrote:

Rumbled!

On Friday at 16:42 Martin replied:

Yeah, she copied me in. Bollocks. Don't suppose you still consider me a genius?

On Friday at 16:46 Ella replied:

No. What is this book whereof she speaks?

On Friday at 16:48 Martin replied:

Nothing. Drop it. Don't mention it to anyone else.

On Friday at 16:56 Ella replied:

Sure. If it's something you're sensitive about I'll leave it alone.

On Friday at 16:57 Ella wrote:

PS Martin wrote a book, Martin wrote a book.
PPS What's it about? Mr and Mrs Socky?

Reading

On Monday at 8:47 Chris wrote:

All right, Mate,
Emily and I were having a chat last night, and we were wondering: would you mind doing a reading at our wedding? Feel free to turn us down.

Chris

On Monday at 9:02 Martin replied:

Sure! Thanks for thinking of me. That would be great. Very flattered. What would you like me to read?
Martin

On Monday at 9:06 Chris wrote:

We were thinking of something from your book?

Re: Reading

On Monday at 9:07 Martin wrote:

Ella!

On Monday at 9:36 Ella replied:

Yes?

On Monday at 9:38 Martin replied:

I asked you not to say anything about my book.

On Monday at 9:39 Ella replied:

I know. I don't have a memory problem.

On Monday at 9:42 Martin replied:

You told Chris!

On Monday at 9:45 Ella replied:

I know. I said I *don't* have a memory problem. Although you do, apparently.

On Monday at 9:47 Martin replied:

But you said you wouldn't tell anyone.

On Monday at 9:50 Ella replied:

No I didn't. Are you sure your memory is OK?

On Monday at 9:55 Martin replied:

I checked. Ha! The magic of email has caught you out. You said 'Sure. If it's something you're sensitive about I'll leave it alone.' You broke your word.

On Monday at 9:59 Ella replied:

Damn, I broke my word. Now I will never be worthy to succeed in my quest for the Holy Grail.

Martin, you forgot emails don't always convey tone. I said 'Sure' sarcastically.

Hope this helps.

Ella

PS What's it about?

On Monday at 10:04 Martin replied:

It's none of your business what it's about.

On Monday at 10:06 Ella replied:

Is it a Mills & Boon?

On Monday at 10:09 Martin replied:

No.

On Monday at 10:13 Ella replied:

Is it a sex book?
i.e. 'Miss Lucy's Punishment', 'She Knew It Was Wrong', not a 'How To ...' Obviously.

On Monday at 10:15 Martin wrote:

No. If you must know, it's a children's book. But it was a bit misconceived, so I abandoned it.

On Monday at 10:16 Ella wrote:

Is it a children's sex book?
Can I read it?

On Monday at 10:19 Martin wrote:

To answer your questions in reverse order: No, and No (eww, what is that?).
But I will tell you what it's about if you promise not to tell anyone else anything about it or ever mention it, allude to it, or indeed allude to the existence of children's literature of any kind in my presence ever again.

On Monday at 10:20 Ella replied:

Sure

On Monday at 10:25 Martin replied:

Well, if you're sitting comfortably, then I'll begin...

Dates

On Monday at 13:02 Barney wrote:

Mate,
You didn't tell me you wrote a book! Can I read it?
Best wishes,
Barney

On Monday at 13:10 Martin wrote:

I don't know. Can you? It's aimed at your reading age, but some of it you might have to get someone to help you with. How come you know?
Martin

P.S. If you're going to write 'Best wishes' I think I prefer the rhyming sign-offs. 'Best wishes' is creepy.

On Monday at 13:27 Barney wrote:

Sorry for the long time it took me to reply. I had to look up some of the words from your email in 'My First Dictionary'.
Ella wrote to me! She didn't say much, just told me there was no hope for us, and to ask you about your book. Is it being published?

On Monday at 13:29 Martin wrote:

No, it's not being published. The fact that its existence is a closely guarded embarrassing secret would make publishing it kind of counter-productive.

Why aren't you more upset about Ella? No offence. It's that when you're depressed you lose that bouncy puppy quality that really gets on my nerves.

Martin

On Monday at 13:45 Barney wrote:

Hooked up with someone last night. Someone really nice who I have a lot more in common with. I would have emailed earlier, but she only left a little while ago.

On Monday at 13:52 Martin wrote:

Someone you 'have a lot more in common with'? Barney, I shudder to think where you found this person...

On Monday at 14:00 Barney replied:

DJ'd an office party on Saturday night. She's a great dancer, really funny too. I think you'd like her.

On Monday at 14:01 Martin wrote:

You never cease to amaze me, Barney. You must emit some kind of pheromone. Next time I'm going out I want to rub myself against you for a long time. Oh, can she DJ?

On Monday at 14:05 Barney replied:

No. Why should she?

On Monday at 14:10 Martin wrote:

You sound perfectly suited. What's her name?

On Monday at 14:11 Barney replied:

Kate Staple. Oh, the weirdest coincidence...

On Monday at 14:15 Martin wrote:

Yeah, yeah, I know. Listen, Barney, I don't want to come on like your dad, but be very careful to use protection. Will explain later.
Ella will no doubt be heartbroken.

On Monday at 14:16 Martin wrote:

Ella, I quote: 'I will tell you what the book is about if you promise not to tell anyone else anything about it or ever mention it or allude to it ever again.'
But somehow Barney knows about it. Barney!
However I spoke to Chris last night, who had spoken to Barney, and he told me something that makes me feel a lot better about things.
Martin

234

On Monday at 14:35 Ella replied:

Martin, I'm not in the mood. Yes, I wrote that. But only knowing that to tell anyone else who cared about your book I would have to make a new friend, introduce them to you, and then tell them.

I can imagine what Barney told Chris and what Chris told you. I don't want to discuss it.

Ella

On Monday at 14:47 Martin replied:

Oh come now, Ella, there's no need to be embarrassed. I think it's sweet you and Barney talked potential kids' names.

On Monday at 15:03 Ella replied:

Martin, seriously, don't.

On Monday at 15:07 Martin replied:

This is a new side to you. And what cute names you suggested!

On Monday at 15:10 Ella replied:

Martin, please, stop.

I think you can tell from the names I suggested that the subtext, at least on my side, was 'Barney, I don't want to reproduce with you.' And that was before he suggested Bradley or Sophia.

On Monday at 15:13 Martin replied:

Oh, really? But I think Robusto, Beef and Bruton are great names for boys. In fact, I may adopt one of them myself in future. And who wouldn't want a daughter called Mercuria, Balthazette or Superia?

Can't wait to tell everyone that the fearsome Ella Tvertko is a BIG SOFTY.

Lots of Love

Robusto Sargent

On Monday at 15:16 Ella replied:

Robusto, I'm not kidding. What is the date today? Is it really the 4th?

On Monday at 15:17 Martin replied:

It is indeed the 4th.

On Monday at 15:18 Ella replied:

Are you sure?

On Monday at 15:20 Martin replied:

Pretty sure. It's written in a little box in the corner of my computer screen. Why?

On Monday at 15:21 Martin replied:

Actually, no need to answer that. Oh shit.

P.S. I'd go with Bruton or Mercuria, if it comes to that.
P.P.S. You'll look great coming down the aisle. Do they do
maternity bridesmaid's dresses? If you need a happy thought,
picture Barney's face.

A Reminder

On Monday at 15:34 Lucy wrote:

Martin, do you know what the date is?

On Monday at 15:44 Martin wrote:

Oh God, not you too. For goodness' sakes, it's written in the corner of your screen.
It's the 4th.
And please, call me Robusto.

On Monday at 15:47 Lucy replied:

Dear Robusto,
What happens every year on the 4th of July? And I don't mean Independence Day.
    Love,
    Lucy

On Monday at 15:50 Martin wrote:

Oh fuckaroo.

On Monday at 15:57 Martin wrote:

Hi Mum!
Bet you thought I'd forgotten! SURPRISE! I hope the parcel

got there safely. If not, I'm sure it will get there tomorrow. I tried ringing but the phone was engaged. That's what you get for being too popular! I'll try again later. Anyway, hope you're having a lovely day, and hope you didn't think I'd forgotten!
Lots of Love
Martin X X X

On Monday at 16:04 Martin wrote:

Hi Ella
It's definitely the 4th.
Robusto

On Monday at 16:08 Ella wrote:

I know. Fucking hell.

On Monday at 16:10 Martin wrote:

I think the brains tend to come from the mother's side of the family, if that makes you feel better. Don't suppose it's what you want to hear, but I forgot my mum's birthday. I feel crap. Think I covered for it, though.

On Monday at 18:11 Stephen Sargent wrote:

Hi, Martin,
Your mother's off the phone now. I think she'd appreciate a call. Flimsy email, by the way. You forgot, didn't you? You get your memory from your mum's side of the family, if that's any consolation to anyone.
Dad

Re: Acklington Stanley

On Tuesday at 10:12 Laura wrote:

This is to remind everyone that tomorrow is the debut gig by Acklington Stanley. No excuses!
Lots of love,

Laura

PS. This includes you, Martin. Would be great if you could come.

\-

On Tuesday at 10:15 Martin replied:

Dear Laura
Would love to come, but I've stapled my balls to a table leg. Don't think I can make it.
Martin

\-

On Tuesday at 10:23 Laura replied:

How awful!
Have you logged it in the accident book?

Laura

\-

On Tuesday at 10:25 Martin replied:

It was no accident.

\-

On Tuesday at 10:28 Laura replied:

Don't be a grouch. Come! I'll dance with you. Bring lots of people, even better. I'll expect to see you there and dancing, even if you have a work-desk in tow ...

Laura

Part Seven
Firkin Hell

A Serious Interlude

Peace and Love

Barney Reveals Some Surprising News

Firkin Hell

On Thursday at 9:15 Emily wrote:

Hope everyone's OK. There were explosions at Edgware Road, King's Cross and Aldgate about half an hour ago. I can't get through to Chris on his mobile.

On Thursday at 9:17 Martin replied:

Jesus, I guess someone really didn't like Acklington Stanley.

On Thursday at 9:46 Chris wrote:

Martin - that's totally inappropriate, mate.

Just got into work due to massive disruption. There was an announcement about a gas leak or something and we all had to get off at Tottenham Court Road. There's a load of ambulances and police cars around the tube opposite where I work.

On Thursday at 9:49 Ella replied:

I'm alright. I'm still in bed, and planning to remain there.

On Thursday at 10:05 Emily wrote:

There's been another explosion. They said something about it being a bus, but I didn't catch where. There are definitely casualties.

On Thursday at 10:12 Martin wrote:

Apologies for earlier insensitivity. Anyone heard from Barney? Is everyone else's phone fucked?

On Thursday at 10:14 Martin wrote:

Sorry, got my email back from Emily's server with a warning about swearing. For FOCK's sake.
Anyone heard from Barney or Ross?
Everyone else's phone PLAYING UP?

On Thursday at 10:15 Ella wrote:

Why would Ross be in the centre?

On Thursday at 10:17 Martin replied:

Long story.

On Thursday at 10:18 Ross wrote:

I'm OK. Phone coming and going - must be everyone ringing around to check people are safe. Oh by the way, Martin, I picked up milk this morning. Not quite on the same operatic scale as everything else that's unfolding, but I knew it would mean a lot to you.

On Thursday at 10:34 Martin wrote:

Hi Sally
Hope you're OK. It sounds pretty serious. Hope David's OK too.
Martin

On Thursday at 10:36 Sally replied:

Yeah, we're both safe. Glad you're all right.
Lots of love
Sally

On Thursday at 10:38 Martin wrote:

Hi Mum
I'm OK - in work at the moment. Everyone here seems to be fine. Phones keep cutting out, if you're trying to get through. It sounds like there have been four explosions, three on the tube and one on a bus. Chris can see stuff from his office and it's a hell of a mess over there. Could you let Dad and Lucy know I'm safe?
Love
Martin

On Thursday at 10:40 Martin wrote:

Barney
When you get this can you reply a.s.a.p. Not sure what's up with phones – someone says the phone lines have been diverted to emergency use only. We're getting a bit worried about you.
Martin

On Thursday at 11:45 Chris wrote:

It looks like bloody Baghdad out the window here. They're bringing up bodies and there are people milling around covered in blood. Loads of smoke and mess. There's someone sitting in reception with their fucking nose hanging off. Definitely not a fucking gas leak.

On Thursday at 12:02 Chris wrote:

For Emily, and those others of you whose servers have kindly refused to deliver my message:

'It looks like BALLY Baghdad out the window here. They're bringing up bodies and there are people milling around covered in blood. Loads of smoke and mess. There's someone sitting in reception with their FLIPPING nose hanging off. Definitely not a FREAKING gas leak.'

Re: Firkin Hell

On Thursday at 12:21 Barney wrote:

Hi All,
I'm OK. Wasn't on usual line due to staying at Kate's house last night. Apparently the whole tube service has shut down, so I guess I'll be trying for the repeat tonight.
Barney

On Thursday at 12:22 Martin wrote:

Well, Barney seems to be taking things in his stride.
Anyone else feeling the tiniest bit tense?

On Thursday at 12:34 Emily replied:

I got through to Chris and he sounds like he's in shock. A girl from his office was on one of the trains. She had FRICKING glass in her hair. I think someone had to suggest to her that she could go home if she wanted.

Everyone here is sitting around wondering what to do and checking the news online.

On Thursday at 12:40 Martin replied:

Not quite sure how anyone's going to get home. Not over-keen to hop on a bus right now, even if there are any.

On Thursday at 13:56 Ella wrote:

If anyone is stuck in central London they are welcome to come over to mine. I'm out of bed now. Pictures on the news look fucking atrocious. Literally.

I think under the circumstances it's not too early to unscrew a bottle. If you guys fancy facing sodding Armageddon pissed, the more the merrier.

Ella

PS Barney, this doesn't mean I'm reconsidering shagging you again.

On Thursday at 14:04 Ross wrote:

Cheers, Ella. I think I just want to get back home. About to join the thousands who've had the same idea.

Martin, I have bad news. I went to the fridge at work and someone has used our milk. We seem to be getting through a lot of caffeinated drinks in the office today.

On Thursday at 14:10 Ella wrote:

Oh for goodness sake. To preserve the purity of Emily's eyes and ears I will rephrase my offer:

'If anyone is stuck in central London they are welcome to come over to mine. I'm out of bed now. Pictures on the news look REALLY RATHER atrocious. Literally.

I think under the circumstances it's not too early to unscrew a bottle. If you guys fancy facing SILLY OLD Armageddon pissed, the more the merrier.

Ella

PS. Barney this still doesn't mean I'm reconsidering COPULATING WITH you again.'

Oh, if anyone wants to hear some good news, I'm not pregnant.

Blitz Spirit

On Friday at 10:00 Sally wrote:

I take it we're all back at our desks?

On Friday at 10:02 Emily replied:

Chris got in all right, eventually. He was pretty determined.
On home email, so you can swear again.

On Friday at 10:04 Martin replied:

Yeah, I came in. Otherwise I'd have had no excuse not to tidy
the flat. Whatcha doing at home, Emily?

On Friday at 10:08 Emily replied:

I have flu. Seriously. Ask Chris.

On Friday at 10:14 Sally wrote:

Must be going around. The office is half empty. Anyone else
about?

On Friday at 10:16 Ross wrote:

Yeah, I kind of had to come in. Martin and I have run out of milk at home. Could buy some, but I still have a quarter of a pint I paid for here, so...

On Friday at 10:18 Martin replied:

From anyone else I'd think that was unflappable British pluck. But I suspect you really are that tight, aren't you?

On Friday at 10:32 Sally replied:

Hmm, David seems to have got this flu that's going around. Chicken flu? I guess theatre needs him.

I had a weird conversation with my gran last night. She said it was like the Blitz. Except of course that during the Blitz the tube was where people went to be safe from bombs. Also, I never understand how people made tights out of gravy. Or indeed why? What was that all about?

How was Ella's?

On Friday at 10:35 Martin replied:

Alas, the end-of-the-world orgy I had envisaged didn't come to pass. We did open the Princess Diana Memorial Brandy she'd been treasuring, though.

On Friday at 10:38 Sally replied:

The stuff in the heart-shaped bottle? How was it?

On Friday at 10:40 Martin replied:

Gone off. Just as well, really, considering we must have been fairly smashed to have even considered it.

Yet another police car with a wailing siren going past at top speed.

Puts it all in perspective, doesn't it?

On Friday at 10:43 Sally replied:

Not really. You're still a twat. But there aren't that many people around. Pint later?

Suggestions

Hey, guys,

Glad to hear everyone's OK. Don't suppose anyone's in the mood to suggest fun or wacky ways to celebrate our mutual friend's impending nuptials?

Mike

Reassured?

On Friday at 13:45 Martin wrote:

Am I the only one to feel less rather than more safe having learned that the high-level group charged with safeguarding us from terrorism is called COBRA? Who came up with that? Austin Powers?

On Friday at 13:56 Sally replied:

It's scary, but probably not in the way they intended.

On Friday at 14:09 Martin replied:

Where do they meet? Hollow dormant volcano? Do they each step into an ordinary-looking postbox or phone booth, go down a shute and then get driven by golf buggy to the Cobradome or whatever they no doubt call it?

On Friday at 14:26 Sally replied:

Possibly they are hoping that the bomb-makers are laughing too hard at the name to do the fiddly bits...

On Friday at 15:03 Chris wrote:

Sorry to break the 'hilarious' mood. They're still looking for bodies opposite where I'm sitting. And it's COBR, anyway.

Re: Re: Acklington Stanley

On Saturday at 14:08 Lucy wrote:

Glad to hear you're alive. It all sounds pretty scary. Take care of yourself, big bro.

PS: Working in the pub is absolutely knackering. Can't be arsed even to transform the semi-psychotic feelings it produces in me into comedy. I swear to God I'm not leaving bed today. Until four o'clock, when I have to go to work. Damn.

PPS: I've emailed Miriam to ask her to bring me a cup of tea. If this works I may never have to leave my bed again.

On Saturday at 14:11 Martin replied:

I appreciate the sentiment, but 'taking care of myself' isn't really going to help if someone decides to blow me up. I mean, I will take a clean hanky and not go out with wet hair, but that almost certainly won't do much good.

Fucking hell, this hangover's pretty scary too. Definitely not leaving the house today. Toying with the idea of ringing the pizza company and ordering something with a paracetemol topping. My liver must be getting old. I seem to be shedding a lot of hair as well. Either it's time for my summer coat or I'm going bald. In divine compensation, however, I'm sprouting a lot of hair from my nose and ears.

On Saturday at 14:13 Lucy replied:

Who were you out with? What are you up to today?

On Saturday at 14:27 Martin replied:

Well I've spent the last half hour deciding whether or not to clip my nails. The backs of my hands are hairy. How long have the backs of my hands been hairy? I don't want hairy hands. I feel like something is going to happen any moment. It's like an existential sense of dread. Mixed with moments when I want to go out and cuddle a puppy and buy balloons.

On Saturday at 14:30 Lucy replied:

Yes, 'existential dread'. Either that or you're hungover. I've warned you about going drinking with that Jean-Paul Sartre ...

On Saturday at 14:35 Martin replied:

I was out with Sally, of all people. It was quite nice. Didn't even make an insane prick of myself. Or try to pull her. Or put a sock on my hand and berate her. No anecdotes to be recounted, really. We had a lot of pints and went home. Believe I had a conversation about Iraq with the taxi driver and we had pretty much established a plan for the future by the time we got back. Alas, I can't remember it.

On Saturday at 14:37 Lucy replied:

Sock??? I won't even ask.
By the way, how were the Stanley? As 'the kids' aren't calling them. Their debut kind of got pushed off the front pages.

On Saturday at 14:40 Martin replied:

I'm a bit low on bile at the moment, so imagine this a lot more vitriolic:

First, think of U2

On Saturday at 14:41 Lucy replied:

If I must.

On Saturday at 14:43 Martin replied:

Well, Acklington Stanley sound a bit like U2. If U2 were all wasps. Playing in a damp matchbox. I thought I had one of their songs stuck in my head the next day, but it turned out to be that thing when you still have water in your ear from the shower.

On Saturday at 14:45 Lucy replied:

So not great? And what's Gwyn like?

On Saturday at 14:48 Martin replied:

Well, most of all he's fat. Not that I have anything against people being fat, except that they're lazy, greedy and they look a bit shit. But he jiggles around on stage and bounces up and down. Which is fine. Except that when he shakes his hips, he stops shaking a long time before his hips do. And one of his flabby tits fell out of his vest at one point. But it's all about the music, man.

And the music is not so hot?

PS: Am I still meant to be adding extra vitriol and toppings of spite?

I'm getting into my stride now. As alleged 'supergroups' go, they were all right. Better than Dalis Car, not as good as Me Me Me.

Listen, if you say 'It's all about the music', the music better be strong enough to distract you from the sight of a heaving white arse peering out at the audience whenever you bend over to pick up your tambourine. I mean, even Mozart wore a wig onstage, for Christ's sake.

The music. More to the point, the songs for Laura. Which I have a hideous suspicion Gwyn considers a 'suite'.

There's one called 'Laura', which is about how nice Laura is, especially to overlook the singer's many failings. Doesn't mention the fact that he's an ugly biffer with a face like a hospital bag of extracted liposuction fat. Contains the lines 'Laura/ I was so cruel/ But you made it all cool.' Or as I sang along 'Laura/ I am a fool/ I am the biggest tool.'

There's 'The Saddest Eyes'. It's about Laura's eyes. Which are, allegedly, 'the saddest'. Only, perhaps, when she's looking at a lardy talentless wanker?

There is the moving ballad 'I Didn't Know', in which Gwyn alleges 'he didn't know he was hurting you' and bawls about Laura 'loving her better'. I heard the second bit as 'loving her batter', which makes sense. Perhaps he was hurting her by lying on top of her when attempting sexual intercourse. Because he is so fucking fat.

There is a song called, I shit you not, 'Lady'. It is also about Laura. Like all songs called 'Lady' it was asinine, mawkish shite.

At that point I went for a very long slash. Nevertheless, through the damp-beaded walls, unable to block my ears due to my hands being otherwise engaged, I could hear Gwyn laryngically bellowing the couplet 'Lady, lady, lady/ Save me, save me, save me.' Fuckin' Shakespeare.

Actually, by that point, he was finally bellowing an emotion with which I connected. I see why they only use plastic glasses at these events.

I'm not even going to get into the acoustic section. For a band who claim The Fall and The Velvet Underground as key influences, they sound surprisingly like a weedier version of Keane.

Acklington Stanley? Armitage Shanks more like.

Didn't get my dance with Laura either.

Glad to get that off my chest.

Lots of Love

Martin

P.S. The Lost Cause were crap as well. In fact they made Acklington Stanley look good, which requires a certain very special kind of genius. They all look about twelve apart from the drummer, who is about 45, wears a big Russian fur hat, and plays a solo in every song. They have a song called 'Roland Barthes', the only lyric of which I caught was: 'I was sitting in the bath/ reading Roland Barthes'. I may be wrong - the sound was pretty poor. Thank God.

On Saturday at 15:10 Lucy replied:

Phew. Not a big fan, then?

PS: Nice of Gwyn to write a song about our dog, though. On the subject of Lady, I got a long email about her health from Mum. Poor little thing.

PPS: Shame you didn't catch the rest of the lyrics to 'Roland Barthes'. How do you follow that couplet? 'Then the phone rang/ it was Giscard D'Estaing'? Except that actually rhymes ...

PPPS: I know he's not a philosopher, but I think he is French.

PPPPS: Oh, of course - 'Driving in my car/ Reading Jacques Derrida'

PPPPPS: 'Sitting on the loo/ Reading Albert Camus'

PPPPPPS: You can't expect every band to be as good as Me Me Me. It's over. Time to move on. Stop hangin' around, bangin' around.

PPPPPPPS: Where is my cup of tea, Miriam? That's it, there's no choice but to get up.

On Saturday at 15:14 Martin replied:

I notice you are using humour in an increasingly threadbare attempt to avoid mentioning Sam. Please tell me that is because you've jettisoned him.

On Saturday at 15:18 Lucy replied:

Damn, was hoping you wouldn't notice that. Yeah, I've been meaning to get round to letting him go, but I've been really busy. And the streams of presents and lavish attention have made it hard to find the appropriate time. He's away on a field trip. I will do it when he gets back.

On Saturday at 15:30 Martin replied:

Sam's off counting pebbles, eh?

Anyway, it's been lovely and a welcome chance to vent, but I must get back to contemplating the fragility of life. Let me know when you have bade Sam take up his kagoule and crayons and fuck off.

Rucksacks

On Wednesday at 9:48 Martin wrote:

Why do they keep talking about the hunt for the 'mastermind' behind the attacks? Does it really take Moriarty to put a bomb in a backpack?

On Wednesday at 10:13 Barney wrote:

Well, I'm not Einstein, but shouldn't they just ban rucksacks from public transport?

They are well sad anyway.

On Wednesday at 10:23 Martin replied:

Thanks, Barney. I think you've penetrated to the heart of the issue.

Although that idea would have the side benefit of keeping bloody backpackers off the tube and preventing them from jamming a load of smelly socks under your nose as they stand on your feet.

On Wednesday at 10:33 Ella replied:

But cheers for clearing up any potential confusion between you and the man who split the atom ...

However, I have been calling for the banning of rucksacks for years, merely on aesthetic grounds.

On Wednesday at 10:45 Barney wrote:

They look shit too.

Joke - Christ guys can you lay off with the 'stupid' comments a bit? I mean I may not be...

Hold on a minute. I'll mail back.

On Wednesday at 10:47 Martin wrote:

Barney?

On Wednesday at 10:48 Ella wrote:

Did he get his finger stuck in the disk drive? Again?

On Wednesday at 10:50 Barney wrote:

Sorry. I couldn't think of any other major intellectual figure that fits the sentence I was trying to write. That was another joke.

Yeah I can - Merleau-Ponty.

There's no need to always be putting me down, just to make yourselves feel better about yourselves. It's not necessary, because I already think you are both smart and funny. Anyway, I may not be the smartest, or even a very good DJ, but I've got a good heart and I'm a loyal friend and that's what matters.

Barney

On Wednesday at 11:02 Ella wrote:

Who told you that? Your mum?

Hi Ella

I should note that those were the first jokes I think Barney has ever made to me. And, moreover, Barney's first ever use of inverted commas.

Do I detect the hand of the new girlfriend here? Give it two weeks and she'll be ripping the piss with the rest of us.
Martin

You might mention to him that you don't have to write 'that was a joke' every time. Although the clarification was helpful in those particular cases. I had almost forgotten how glad I am not to be bearing his child.

Peace and Love

Dear Colleagues,

As you know, last Thursday London was the target of
a terrorist outrage. MediaSolutions takes the safety of our
employees very seriously, and you will have noticed that security
checks have now been instituted in the reception area.

After much discussion about the proper response to the
events of last Thursday, it has been decided to establish a new
electronic bulletin board for the benefit of those employees who
wish to share their thoughts and feelings in the aftermath of this
tragedy. Perhaps you would like to talk about how the attacks
affected you, to describe how your life has changed since the
bombings, or perhaps to share messages of hope.

Comments may be made anonymously.

Please report any misuse of this board to Martin Sergeant in
the IT Department.

Simon Tapper, Head of Security

Martin Sergeant, IT

- I want to say that what happened has shocked me to the core.
  I never thought anything like this could happen to us. I feel so
  lucky to be alive. [Sarah H]
- I feel so angry, not only with the terrorists, but with our
  leaders who misled us and failed to keep us safe [Andy T]
- I never thought I'd feel unsafe walking the streets of London
  [Luke J]
- You used to feel safe walking the streets of London? You don't
  live around where I'm from then. [anonymous]
- Anyone want to buy a bike? Good condition, £75 quid o.n.o.

includes pump. [please contact Phil Thornhill in Accounts]

- When I look at pictures of the people who died, I realise what a diverse, talented society we live in. We must all work to cherish that, otherwise the terrorists really have won. [Claire G]
- I'm so proud of how Londoners have pulled together to show the world what we are made of. I think we all deserve a pat on the back. [Ben J]
- Apart from the terrorists, of course, who may well also have been Londoners. [anonymous]
- I still can't believe what is happening. It could have been any one of us. [Matthew B]
- Not Martin Sergeant. He sleeps in the office 'cos his girlfriend chucked him out. [anonymous]
- I feel nervous every time I take a bus or tube. [Mary W]
- I moved carriages twice today because I was suspicious of foreign-looking people. [anonymous]
- I would like to express my deepest sympathies to those who lost their lives, and send my thoughts to their families in this terrible time. What drove these killers was not religion but hate. [Feisal M]
- I think we need to look at the deeper causes behind the actions of last Thursday, and ask ourselves: Were we to blame? [Charlie D]
- Charlie, I think that's nonsense. I think the people who did the bombings were to blame, and we shouldn't seek to excuse them. [Petra V]
- Petra, to understand is not to condone. I think we should ask whether our actions in the Middle East have made the situation better or worse. [Charlie D]
- What, because I didn't go on the anti-war march I deserve to die? Cheers, Charlie [Petra V]
- I think you would have died even if you had, Petra, if you were in the wrong place at the wrong time. These people are sick. [Stuart F]
- I think we need less understanding, not more. I'm sickened when people try to justify these terrible actions. We've been

too understanding for too long. [anonymous]

- Why post anonymously, unless you're embarrassed by what you think? [Hamid A]
- How has anyone's life changed since last Thursday? [Elizabeth J]
- I've started learning Arabic. [anonymous]
- I don't sit next to foreigners on the tube [Pierre S]
- I think he means *other* foreigners. [anonymous]
- I think that attitude is really unhelpful, Pierre. We should all realise that not every Muslim is a terrorist. Lots of them have condemned the attacks and are as horrified as we are. [Sarah G]
- Thank you, Sarah G. The more people learn about Islam the more they will see that it's nothing to do with terrorism. [Hamid A]
- I don't take the tube any more. [Michael B]
- Well, lucky you being able to walk in to work. 'Oh no, I'm not going to die screaming underground with the plebs, 'cos I can afford to live on the edge of Zone One.' And your FIRKIN trainers stink, Michael. Could you start leaving them in reception? Or preferably outside the building? [anonymous]
- What this has taught me is that we need to start taking pride in being British again. It is a privilege to live in this country with its great history. We should be teaching all our kids to be PROUD of being British. God knows, we have given a lot to the world: Shakespeare, democracy, the Industrial Revolution, the Beatles and the flushing toilet, to name but five things. [Barry H]
- Yeah, not to mention the Empire, the package holiday and Pop Idol. Democracy was the Greeks, by the way. [Oli E]
- Just one of their great inventions. [Andrew D]
- Which definitely don't include the modern flushing toilet. Never going back to Corfu again. [Luke G]
- Actually, that is ignorant. There were toilets in the palace at Knossos over three thousand years ago, when the English were wiping their bums with peat. [Aris K]
- I think the toilets in our hotel were older than that, Aris. [Luke G]

- Fascinating. Did they appear to have ever been 'excavated'? [Oli E]
- OK. Has anyone else got anything to say ON THE SUBJECT FOR WHICH THIS NOTICEBOARD WAS SET UP? Anyone made any resolutions or noticed any changes about themselves? [Sarah G]
- I feel like everyone is staring at me on the tube. I've started leaving my rucksack at home, and yesterday I even thought about whether my beard was really necessary. I've never felt like this in England before. [anonymous]
- I've given up drinking. [anonymous]
- I've started drinking again. [Steve B]
- I've started pilfering things from my employers and colleagues. [anonymous]
- Yeah, we noticed, Luke [Laura M].
- I had a wank in the work toilets yesterday. Didn't want to die horny. [anonymous]
- You used to do that before, Luke (again). What was your excuse then? [Laura M]
- I've decided to come out to my family, friends, and colleagues in the IT department. [Martin Sergeant]
- Congratulations! [Andrew D]
- That's really brave of you, Martin. Of course, we all knew. Best wishes for the future. I hope you'll be very happy. But surely you should have mentioned this to Charlotte G first? Do it now - she's on the way to your office looking pretty unimpressed. [Martin Sargent]
- I didn't write that. That message is going to be removed and this noticeboard will shortly be temporarily suspended, due to its misuse at the hands of a few immature people. Any subsequent misuse will result in the messageboard being shut down permanently and without further warning. [Martin Sergeant]
- Also, can people please stop reporting misuses of the board to me? I'm the other Martin Sargent and I'm really not that bothered. To those who congratulated me on coming out, that's the other Martin too. Still, much appreciated. [Martin Sargent]

- 'Misuse at the hands of immature people'? Sounds like a great night out for some. Arf arf. [anonymous]
- Being homosexual has no connection to paedophilia, and is nothing to be ashamed of. [Sarah G]
- Being immature has no connection to age. And you made the connection, Sarah G. Although of course they're both Greek inventions ... [anonymous]
- That is another very ignorant comment. [Aris K]
- Nobody mind Aris, he's still upset since he found out about Alexander the Great. [anonymous]
- Oh I know what's changed. What happened to all the articles about 'How to Spot a Chav'? [Laura M]
- They're being rewritten as 'How to Spot a Suicide Bomber' [Oli E]
- I think some people who have posted on this noticeboard are really sick. It's an insult to those who died. [Sarah H]
- Hi, Sarah. I don't think anyone has posted anything that insults the dead, although the usual blend of thinly-veiled homophobia, Islamophobia and racism that infects our society is fully displayed. I think it's important to recognise that humour is the way some people deal with events that they otherwise could not deal with. [Hamid A]
- I agree with Hamid A. I also think it's a tragedy that everyone's refusal to accept Martin's decision has scared him back into the closet. [Martin Sargent]
- I agree with Hamid A. We should remember that the British sense of humour is part of what makes this country GREAT Britain. [Ben J]
- I agree with Ben J and Hamid A. If we stop laughing, the terrorists have won. [Sarah H]
- Umm, no. Surprisingly the British sense of humour has never been mentioned as a target by any terrorist group. I think the terrorists have 'won' if they establish a Global Caliphate based on a strict interpretation of certain aspects of Islamic law. [anonymous]
- Or if we stopped interfering ILLEGALLY in the Middle East, acted to enforce Israel's adherence to UN regulations and used

our global influence to build a better, fairer world. [Charlie D]
- Is anybody in this building planning on doing any work today?
  [Laura M]

Thursdays

On Thursday at 12:44 Martin wrote:

OK, now I really am terrified.

On Thursday at 13:01 Ella replied:

Damn. Why are they bombing on Thursdays? Thursday is singles' night at my local Sainsbury's.

On Thursday at 13:13 Martin replied:

What happened to the Alpha Course guy?

On Thursday at 13:15 Ella replied:

Oh, he turned out to be trying to save me.
That was not a misspelling.

PS Oh Martin, you're at your desk at lunchtime? Sweet. What is in your sandwiches? Did Ross make them for you?
PPS Sorry, forgot to call you by your new nickname. Mr Prickles.

On Thursday at 13:18 Martin replied:

I've been called worse. But I still prefer Robusto.

On Thursday at 14:25 Barney wrote:

Dear Martin and Ella,

It may surprise you to learn that I have been accepted on an MA course starting in September. Ha!

Now I have to tell my boss...

Best wishes,

Barney

On Thursday at 14:35 Ella replied:

You're right, Barney. That does surprise me.

But congratulations.

Ella

On Thursday at 14:36 Ella wrote:

Well, Mr Prickles, what do you make of that? I guess I unlocked something in the boy.

What happened to Barney's rhyming sign-offs? I rather liked those.

Ella

On Thursday at 14:40 Martin replied:

DJ Idiot, Master of Arts? That's it. The world really has gone mad.

P.S. Don't call me Mr Prickles.

Part Eight
Normal Service Resumes

Stag Night Plans • Hairy Hands
The Saddest Hedgehog
The Beard Gag Explained

Re: Suggestions

On Wednesday at 18:04 Mike wrote:

Dear Mates-of-Chris,

All the suggestions for the stag night are in and have been given due consideration. I got a lot of useful feedback. As well as some that were ... not so helpful. I'm sorry to have to disappoint those who suggested: a watercolouring class; antenatal support sessions for dads; hiring a dead-eyed Latvian 'masseuse' for Chris and watching through a two-way mirror; doing a tour of historical East End crime scenes; or 'putting Chris in a big box and sending him, nude, to Alaska'. Actually, only one person will be disappointed, since all those suggestions were provided by Martin. Luckily I was expecting that.

Various people suggested: go-karting; going to a dry ski slope; going sailing or going paint-balling. I should perhaps have clarified that this event is meant to celebrate/mourn Chris getting married, rather than turning 15.

Karaoke was considered, but Chris was a little worried about one of our number 'doing a repeat of last time', and we weren't sure which karaoke bars he is barred from. (Martin, again).

Throwing convention to the wind, I have asked Chris himself what his ideal evening would involve. With typical adventurousness he replied, 'Pub, curry, pub, club. Not getting tied to anything naked.' I think the nudity bit refers to him, as opposed to our tying a clothed Chris to something or someone in a state of undress.

Anyway, the final, provisional, tentative plan is this: a cruise up the river to admire our magnificent city, dinner, then on to a club. Suggestions for club venues still being considered. I rang around a few places to check they accepted stag nights. A surprising number of people hung up on me.

I've attached a possible schedule and a map to find the meeting place, in case any of you can't find the Thames without one. Mark the date in your diaries in big red letters and dust off your fake plastic breasts.

See you all then,

Mike

PS - Barney, I'm afraid Emily is using the flat that night for her hen night. Sorry, 'bachelorette evening'. Not that I think Chris would be amused if we were to 'bust in, crap on the floor and mess everything up to make it look like he's been burgled'. Chris has, seriously, requested that we keep a lid on the seething homosocial psychosis that characterises the average stag night. Or as the man himself put it: 'If you guys stitch me up, I will hunt you down and make you suffer.'

Re: Re: Re: Acklington Stanley

On Wednesday at 12:02 Gwyn wrote:

Dear Friends and Fans (of Acklington Stanley),

We'd like to extend our apologies to those who managed to struggle across London for our recent show at the Falcon. Unfortunately, as you know, Johnno our bassist was stranded in Greenwich, and Jez our drummer decided not to show up. We hope those who did make it enjoyed the acoustic set. Those people who wanted their money back should contact the box office.

First some bad news: due to events beyond our control, Acklington Stanley have been forced to cancel our series of 'guerrilla gigs' around the capital.

Now for some good news (at last!): we have more shows coming up. Dates and locations to be announced shortly!

Now for some more good news: from a selection of press clippings we have gleaned the following items:

'Acklington Stanley […] have all the makings of a band who are going places' [www.gigsonline.com]

'their sound evokes the glacial majesty of peak period U2' [*Camden Gazette*]

'Could Acklington Stanley be the new new new Coldplay?' [www.jewishherald.com; see the print edition for a rather fetching photo of us in Mark's mum's garden!]

'The lead singer is f*cking sexy' [www.laurasblog.com]

And a big 'fuck off' to the man from the *NME* who never showed up.

Look forward to seeing you all at the upcoming gigs

Gwyn, Johnno, Mark (and Jez, if he can be bothered to show. Drum machines ain't expensive mate)

279

On Thursday at 12:15 Martin wrote:

Hi Laura

Glad to see the Stanley aren't letting the terrorists win. What a blow for freedom they're striking.

I don't know if it was accidental, but Gwyn left out the telling central bit of that quote from www.gigsonline.com, which reads in full: 'Acklington Stanley, *despite being comprised of graduates of third-string no-hopers Fork, Overpass and Mucky Faces, as well as the bald drummer from tuneless jazz-funk noodlers Herbalessence (known round these parts as "Guffbucket")*, have all the makings of a band going places.' Oh yes, and it continues, 'This reviewer hopes that the place they are going is far far away, and that they stay there for ever.'

I wasn't aware that the *Camden Gazette* employed wasps as reviewers.

As for Gwyn being sexy, the mind reels…

Martin

On Thursday at 12:18 Laura wrote:

Wasps???

Re: Pretty in Pink

Hey Ella

How was the fitting session with the bridesmaids? I hear
Emily designed the dresses herself, so they can't be that bad. Can
they?

Martin

Yeah. Unfortunately I suspect she designed them when she
was twelve. I won't be surprised if she arrives at the church
riding My Little Pony. The whole experience was excruciating.
I kept expecting Jeremy Beadle to pop out and reveal it was a
wind-up. Sadly, he didn't.

What can I say without being too mean? Probably nothing.
Ballerina Barbie would be embarrassed to be seen in this get-up.
The dresses turn out to be not just pink, but a variety of pinks.
A variety of pinks that clash not only with each other, but with
the complexion of human skin. I don't know whether this was
intentional. Maybe Emily kept running out of felt-tips when she
was doing the original design. Apparently I look sweet. Great. If
I wanted to look sweet, I'd turn up dressed as Pikachu. Thank
God someone managed to dissuade Emily from the bonnet idea,
but she wouldn't be budged on the ruffles and bows. I look like
Barbara Cartland's truffle-box. And an idiot. The whole thing is
so Freudian.

Stop. Laughing.

PS Obviously this is all strictly *entre nous*. Emily is already cross at me for asking 'Why do I have to be Mr Pink?' in my best Steve Buscemi voice.

On Thursday at 12:32 Martin replied:

Freudian? Well, if nothing else, this explains why Chris is wearing that skin-tight pink bodysuit and the fuzzy shoes.

I wasn't laughing. I was enjoying picturing you dressed as Pikachu.

As it happens, I'm feeling somewhat weirded. I found something odd on the internet while I was googling Laura.

On Thursday at 12:35 Ella replied:

Let me guess. Was it some girls, covered in goo?

On Thursday at 12:40 Martin replied:

No, actually it's much more disturbing than that.

Laurasblog

I've been reading www.laurasblog.com. She has the same first name as you. Wow, she even works in this building. That's really eerie. God, I don't think much of that M. guy she was thinking about seeing. I quote:

'As you guys know, I don't really go for conventionally handsome.'

'I think M. may be going a bit bald. Noticed the light reflecting off his forehead as he was typing today.'

'Not sure if he's yet another self-obsessed wannabe-hipster.'

'I noticed at lunch today that M. has hairy hands! Gross!!! Have to do something about that.'

'His ex has done a real number on him. Do I really want to hook up with someone with "damaged goods" stamped on his forehead?'

You're holding an online poll on the subject??? And pass on my thanks to Sandra from Texas, who thinks I sound like 'bad news, girl' and then compares me to a boyfriend who ended up in prison for stealing her car drunk. The only sense on the whole site is the recent comment from Johannes Jester: 'I should inform the voters that Gwyn is a talentless tedious whiner who takes the already debased medium of rock and roll to previously unimagined new lows. And Martin is not going bald. Also Laura has slightly protruding googly eyes which under certain circumstances can appear somewhat unnerving.'

I am not a 'wannabe' hipster.

I wash my hairy hands of you.

Martin

P.S. Let me know how the poll turns out. I predict a late surge.

Thanks for ignoring me at lunch.

Sorry about the weblog - I started it before I got to know you. If you scroll back you may notice that I've been interested in you for a long time.

The poll's meant to be a bit of fun, by the way, so you can stop trying to rig it.

Oh, didn't see you at lunch. I have to concentrate because my hairy hands make it a bit difficult to carry my tray. Or perhaps I was dazzled by the reflected glare of the canteen lights coming off my cranium. Or perhaps I thought you were looking at someone else with your enormous distended eyes.

Like I'd stoop to rigging your stupid poll. Don't flatter yourself.

By the way, Acklington Stanley: they look like crap, sound like crap, and probably smell like crap. If I had to think of one word to sum them up, do you know what it would be? Clue: it comes out of your backside. I'm praying for a Jazzbucket reunion. And Gwyn can put that on his next flyer.

I've been meaning to ask if you can shed any light on how Gwyn comes up with his lyrics. Does he write them in some other language (possibly Finnish) and translate them using babelfish.com? That's all I can come up with to explain lines like 'Now it's plunder regency/ Look out pandemonium pandemic' and the grammatically and biologically baffling 'Here we were, I stand/ In my heart and out of my head.' He then announces he has 'something he needs to say to you', which turns out to be 'I can't turn around'. Well, I'm hardly surprised given the circumstances. May I speculate via which orifice he entered his

284

own torso? And if he will insist on partly acting-out his words in bad mime, you might suggest he takes steps to prevent his bingo wings flapping around. Oh, and be sure to mention that 'Cancel my subscription/ To televised affliction', apart from making no sense, doesn't bloody rhyme. Even if delivered with a furrowed brow and in a 'meaningful' voice. So there.

On Thursday at 14:07 Martin wrote:

Hi guys
You can ignore the text about the poll. I've been rumbled.
Martin

On Thursday at 14:11 Sally replied:

Wow, Martin, she realises things about you that I took years to notice. I voted for Gwyn. By the way, thanks for telling her so much about us. You didn't mention Mr Socky, I notice. Or the clothes thing. Or your book.

On Thursday at 14:14 Martin replied:

Sally, would it surprise you to learn that I didn't realise she was going to pass on our conversations to the world at large? Nor indeed to speculate whether my maternal grandfather was 'also a slaphead'.

On Thursday at 14:15 Sally replied:

Reading on.
What the fuck? 'Martin's ex sounds like a real maniac. That fucking play was like being trapped during a riot at an Institution for the Criminally Talentless. Thank God Martin

thought so too, otherwise all bets would be well and truly off. Still, hard to forgive the person responsible for dragging me to that traduction of the very concept of "entertainment". To read more of what I thought, check out www.yourtheatre.com.'

Well, it's hard to act when you are getting blinded by the reflection off someone's bonedome and you can't tell where the girl sitting next to them is looking with her freaky Marty Feldman eyes. When you see her again knock her other contact lens out for me.

PS - Sandra from Texas suggests you 'shave your hands and put it on your head'. Worth thinking about.

On Thursday at 14:18 Laura wrote:

You should be more careful about flinging the personal comments about, if you can't handle it being directed at you.
You're not that tall, by the way.
Or thin.

On Thursday at 14:20 Martin replied:

Yeah, good comeback. That's one in the eye for me. You psycho.

On Thursday at 15:00 Ella wrote:

Martin, out of interest, what upsets you most about this sorry but fascinating affair? Is it
a) the invasion of your privacy
b) the accurate but ungallant physical observations
c) the unsurprising revelation that you obsessively bitch out your supposed 'mates' to a comparative stranger
d) the assertion that you are a 'wannabe' hipster

e)   the fact that you are trailing in the poll by a considerable margin?

By the way, Laura has updated her readers with the latest news. I suppose the fact she calls herself Laura M (understandably) meant that you didn't pick up on this at an earlier stage, when you no doubt 'googled' her. So to speak.

On Thursday at 15:13 Chris wrote:

Hey, Baldie,

Do you want us to vote in the new poll as well? She's taking suggestions as to what to do now. Willing to write in for you, since I know those hairy hands of yours make it hard to type. Take it easy, Teenwolf.

See you at the stag.

Chris

On Thursday at 15:16 Ross wrote:

Hi Martin,

Glad to see that the readers of www.laurasblog.com have been treated to a hugely exaggerated account of the state of my bedroom and some potentially libellous material about my alleged unwillingness to buy milk.

By the way, I voted for Laura's next move to be 'Get Gwyn to hit you with a hammer.'

Cheers 'mate',

Ross

On Thursday at 15:23 Barney wrote:

'From the invention of the wheel to Barney at the decks, intellectual history has come full circle, if not actually changed direction.' You arrogant wanker.

I voted for Laura to put her recording of you singing 'You Were Always on My Mind' online.
Barney

On Thursday at 15:45 Martin Sergeant wrote:

Hi, Martin,
Hope your day is going well. I've been helping some of the staff get used to using the internet. Of course, most of us have been following things online for months. Wouldn't want to be you during your 'security check' tomorrow. Simon's off to buy some 'special gloves'. I hope he doesn't borrow Benita's rings too. Ouch! Oh yeah, she says to tell you that you can empty your own bin from now on.
Best wishes,
Martin

On Thursday at 16:00 Martin Sargent wrote:

Guys
I think we may be losing sight of who's the victim here.
Martin

P.S. It's me, by the way.
P.P.S. Still time to vote in the poll, unless you want to see me hit with a hammer.

On Thursday at 16:45 Martin Sargent wrote:

I'm serious, guys. Hello? Anyone still speaking to me?

On Thursday at 16:52 Ella replied:

Well, I think you've certainly dispelled those claims that you're 'self-obsessed'...

Mr Prickles

On Monday at 9:04 Barney wrote:

I'm thinking about forgiving you. On one condition.

On Monday at 9:15 Martin replied:

Barney, for the last time, I will NEVER be DJ Idiot's pet dancing fool. Not even if I do get to dress as a scary clown.
Why not ask Ms Staple?

On Monday at 9:20 Barney replied:

She said no too. Dammit. I need a gimmick to set me apart. Kate's on holiday.

On Monday at 9:23 Martin replied:

Barney, trust me. Your sound is distinctive enough without gimmicks. No one is ever going to forget having experienced a set by DJ Idiot.
Where has she gone?

On Monday at 9:26 Barney replied:

Thanks. I think. Kate says DJ Idiot may give people the wrong impression about me.

She's gone off to Greece with her mate Martin.

On Monday at 9:28 Martin replied:

Martin Sergeant? Barney, you do know about their past, right?
What did she suggest as an alternative name? DJ Clever? DJ
MA? DJ Holiday Cuckold?

On Monday at 9:34 Barney replied:

Yeah, I know. I'm not exactly over the moon about it. But
it was booked weeks ago, and apparently nothing's going to
happen. We'll have to wait and see.

On Monday at 9:36 Martin replied:

Bummer for you, but that does mean that at least one of my
enemies is going to be out of the way. Hope Simon Tapper goes
on holiday soon. Climbing up the fire-escape to get to my desk
without a security check in the morning is wearing thin quite
quickly.

On Monday at 9:40 Barney replied:

Martin, have you ever considered that you might be a bit
paranoid? Perhaps you don't have lots of 'enemies'. Perhaps
there are loads of people who go through a whole day without
thinking at all about Martin Sargent.

On Monday at 9:42 Martin replied:

Are you trying to make me paranoid about being paranoid?

Trust me, I have considered the possibility that there's no one out to get me, and people to whom my existence is of little or no concern. But then again, that's exactly what you'd want me to think if you were out to get me, isn't it?

Besides, the Laurasblog episode has perhaps unsurprisingly not diminished my paranoia.

On which note, what is this 'condition' on which my forgiveness depends?

On Monday at 9:45 Barney replied:

Tell me what your book is about.

On Monday at 9:52 Martin replied:

I'm afraid I don't value your friendship that much. Sorry. Why do you care?

On Monday at 9:54 Barney replied:

I care because I want to know why you're freaking out about it. Tell me. Is it about me?

On Monday at 9:55 Martin replied:

It's a full-length book, Barney. I think you are pretty much summed up on a flyer saying 'DJ Idiot'.

On Monday at 10:01 Barney replied:

Is it about a gingerbread man who gets left in the pantry and gets so hungry he eats himself?

On Monday at 10:08 Martin replied:

What? Why on earth would it be?

Umm, if Kate told you that's what happened to your gingerbread man, she may not have as high a regard for your intelligence as you think.

On Monday at 10:13 Barney replied:

Because I know your book is a kids' book, and I was trying to think of the kind of thing I'd write if I was trying to make up a story for kids.

On Monday at 10:15 Martin replied:

Remind me when the time comes never to let you babysit my kids.

OK OK OK. If only to stop any more stupid suggestions on those lines, and because no one else has offered to forgive me, I'll tell you. But you have to swear that it goes absolutely no further than you.

On Monday at 10:20 Barney replied:

I swear on my record box that I will not tell anyone what you are about to confide. Now spill the beans. What is your book about?

On Monday at 10:23 Martin replied:

It's about fifty pages.

On Monday at 10:28 Barney replied:

Martin, how many people called you, emailed you or invited you out this weekend? I estimate approximately none. Unless you're enjoying your new status as a hermit, tell me what your book is about.

On Monday at 10:30 Martin replied:

It's about a hedgehog called Mr Prickles.

On Monday at 10:31 Barney replied:

And?

On Monday at 10:34 Martin replied:

And nothing. That's what it's about. He has an adventure. That's it. End of.

On Monday at 10:38 Barney replied:

It sounds rubbish.

On Monday at 10:49 Martin replied:

What, is that a trick to get me pissed off so I tell you?
No, can't be. You didn't write 'This is a trick' after it.
Fine: Mr Prickles is a lonely hedgehog, who lives, obviously, in a hedge.
He goes looking for love, and keeps thinking he has found it. But he is wrong.

Then he dies.

On Monday at 10:54 Barney replied:

Great, sounds perfectly aimed at that 4-7 market. What's the message?

On Monday at 11:00 Martin replied:

It's shit being a hedgehog.
And by the way, kids, hedgehogs aren't sweet, they're fucking rats with spikes on and they're crawling with fleas.
I had a lot of fun with the illustrations.

On Monday at 11:03 Barney replied:

It's an important message for us all, I think. How does Mr Prickles die?

On Monday at 11:07 Martin replied:

He gets squished, but it's a little more complicated than that. Do you really still want to hear about it?

On Monday at 11:10 Barney replied:

Actually, mate, I lost interest quite a while ago. I think if you don't mind I'm going to play poker online for a bit. Maybe even do some work, catch up with my correspondence. Glad we're mates again.
Oh, go on and tell me, since you're obviously secretly dying to.

On Monday at 11:26 Martin replied:

Right. Mr Prickles, the lonely hedgehog, gets sick of having no one to play with. So he crawls out of his hedge one night when everyone is asleep, and goes to look for a special hedgehog friend.

On the silvery lawn he sees a bowl of milk the kids have left out for him. And when he goes to investigate, he sees the moon's face reflected in it. He thinks 'What a pretty face', and goes to lick it. The milk ripples and he thinks the face is winking at him, so he goes on licking.

But soon he has licked up all the milk, and the face has gone.

Then he sees a garden gnome fishing in the pond. So he goes and sits next to it. And he quite likes that, and the gnome is smiling and wearing his jaunty hat and everything. Mr Prickles asks him if he's caught anything, but the gnome ignores him. After a while he decides the gnome is pretty boring, so the search goes on.

He goes into the house through the catflap. There's a fridge humming, and he thinks it's talking to him, so he goes over and sits by it. But it doesn't answer any of his questions, so he decides it's only interested in talking to itself, and he goes upstairs.

He goes into the little girl's bedroom, and there, in the moonlight spilling onto the desk, he sees... her! His soulmate! Another hedgehog.

He climbs up onto the desk, and it's a struggle, but after various trials and tribulations he gets there. And she is the most beautiful hedgehog he has ever seen. So he snuggles up to her, but she's all cold and doesn't respond to him. Then it gets a bit lighter and he realises he has fallen in love with a hairbrush.

Bitterly disappointed, he climbs down again, and goes outside. He starts wandering along the road, and he's hanging his head, and thinking about what a sham love is, when suddenly he sees the most gorgeous face in the world, lying there in front of him. He smiles at it, and it smiles back. And he sits there for ages, perfectly happy. Of course, it's really his own reflection in a puddle.

Then a milk-float comes along and runs him over.
THE END

On Monday at 11:49 Barney wrote:

That's beautiful. So it's about how you have to learn to love yourself before you can love anyone else?

On Monday at 11:50 Martin replied:

No, Barney. It's about a horny hedgehog.
I'm thinking of calling it *It's Hard to Masturbate When You Have Claws*.

Re: Re: Sam

On Tuesday at 10:12 Elizabeth Sargent wrote:

Dear Martin,

I got a text from Lucy - she's broken up with Sam. I hope she's not too upset, the poor thing. Will ring her when I get out of my meeting.

How was your weekend? Sorry not to call, I was taking Lady to the vet and your dad to the barber, and the weekend just went.

Lots of love,

Mum

PS: What is the 'beard gag'?

On Tuesday at 10:13 Martin wrote:

Hi Lucy

I heard the good news. Hooray! At last.

And it was the beard gag that did it?

Or did you get out an Ordinance Survey and show him where to go?

Lots of Love

Martin

On Tuesday at 10:41 Lucy replied:

Hey Martin,

Yes, I'm free at last. Eventually.

But the beard gag didn't work. Unbelievable, I know.

We were in the pub last night, and the subject came up. OK, I brought it up. And then, of course, I was compelled to do the gag. But all he said was 'Didn't nanny ever tell you personal comments are odious?' And went on with his pint.

He's right, you know.

Lucy

On Tuesday at 10:44 Martin wrote:

The obvious response to that comment would surely be: 'I find you odious, you big patronising beardy Sloane. Take your supposed personality and your hairy back and go and find some traffic to count.' But if that wasn't it, how did you get rid of him?

Martin

On Tuesday at 11:02 Lucy wrote:

Well, call me crazy, but I decided not to go into a tempest of anger and venom and then subside into self-loathing isolation. I just told him, 'I think we are on different journeys, and this is where our paths have to part. I hope there is no bitterness and that we can still be friends.'

On Tuesday at 11:05 Martin replied:

Have I taught you nothing? And that was that?

On Tuesday at 11:10 Lucy replied:

Not exactly. He responded by saying that he felt I'd been trying to push him away for a long time, and asking why I was afraid of love.

On Tuesday at 11:12 Martin replied:

At which point you hit him with an ashtray?

On Tuesday at 11:14 Lucy replied:

No, at which point I said I thought life was all about learning and helping people to grow, and that I thought we had learned all we were going to learn together and we had to grow apart now.

On Tuesday at 11:16 Martin replied:

At which point he hit you with an ashtray?

On Tuesday at 11:19 Lucy replied:

No. At which point he said he wasn't sure I was strong enough to stand alone yet.
Which was when I hit him with the ashtray. Fucking twat.
But how was your weekend?

On Tuesday at 11:22 Martin replied:

Well, no one's talking to me, because Laura turned out to be keeping an intimate diary of our relationship online and it revealed that I slag people off behind their backs. I don't know why everyone's upset - it's not like I don't slag them off to their faces too.
Anyway, I've been moping around having a long dark weekend of the soul. Welcome to being single. It's completely shit.

300

On Tuesday at 11:30 Lucy replied:

Yeah, I can see that people might be upset. But don't worry, you're catching up in the poll.

On Tuesday at 11:32 Martin replied:

Oh, you know about that? Thanks for your vote.

On Tuesday at 11:33 Lucy replied:

Yeah, I emailed Sally to say good luck moving house and she mentioned it.

PS: What makes you assume I voted for you?

On Tuesday at 11:35 Martin replied:

Sally's moving house?

On Tuesday at 11:36 Martin wrote:

You email Sally?

On Tuesday at 11:40 Lucy replied:

Well, I assumed you knew that Sally was moving, since you are supposedly friends again. Sally emailed to invite me to the play, and I emailed back, and we've been in touch ever since.

On Tuesday at 11:43 Martin replied:

But she cheated on me!

On Tuesday at 11:55 Lucy replied:

Bloody hell, Martin. 'Rock and Roll Heart'? The sock thing?
I mean, you're my brother and that, but I can kind of see where
she was coming from. You did write a book in which she appears
as a hairbrush. That's pretty mean.

On Tuesday at 12:01 Martin replied:

You didn't think to mention it to me?

On Tuesday at 12:05 Lucy replied:

Surprisingly, I thought you might overreact.

On Tuesday at 12:14 Martin replied:

I'm not overreacting. I'm going to tell Mum Sam dumped you
because you blow sailors for cash and are addicted to smack.
Judas.

On Tuesday at 12:18 Martin wrote:

Hi Mum
Lucy sounds fine. It sounds like it was her idea and all went
reasonably amicably. She may have hit him with an ashtray at
one point, but I'm hoping that was a joke. Did you know she's
in touch with Sally? Who is apparently moving. Not that she

mentioned it to me. I guess David got that job directing Gilbert and Sullivan in Hell.

In response to your queries:

I had a fairly quiet weekend. Everyone seemed to be away. Had a very restful time chilling out in the flat.

The beard gag is a masterpiece of my own devising. Feel free to use it. It's straightforward but effective. You see someone you know who is growing a beard. You point at it and say, 'Beered?' quizzically. They reply, 'Yes.' And you say, 'Yeah, you must have been.' Works a treat, but it doesn't look so good in print...

Lots of Love

Martin

On Tuesday at 14:56 Elizabeth Sargent replied:

What do you do if they just tell you to bugger off? Sometimes I worry about you, Martin.

Re: Mr Prickles

On Wednesday at 11:24 Barney wrote:

Am I the gnome?

On Wednesday at 11:25 Martin replied:

No, Barney. The gnome never talks. But you could try to be like him if you want...

On Wednesday at 11:26 Barney wrote:

Is Sally the hairbrush?

On Wednesday at 11:27 Martin replied:

Why does everyone think that?

Yes, Barney, you're right. You have intuitively grasped my creative method. I decided to write a book in which my then-girlfriend appears as a hairbrush. Can you see where I got the idea? It's because Sally is made of wood and has thick bristles entirely covering one side of her.

Listen, let me explain something to you about my craft. No one in a book is just someone you know. You take bits and pieces from lots of people and distil them into an imaginary character.

For example, I took your astonishing shallowness, and depicted that as a saucer full of milk.

304

Do you see what I'm saying?

On Wednesday at 11:29 Barney replied:

I see. So if the milk had been sour and thin-skinned, it would have been a self-portrait?

PS are you the hedgehog?

On Wednesday at 11:31 Martin replied:

Yes, that's right, I am. Because whichever way I turn I'm surrounded by pricks.

The Eyes of Laura Mutton

On Wednesday at 12:01 Martin wrote:

Hi Laura,
Don't suppose you fancy lunch?
Martin

On Wednesday at 12:15 Laura replied:

What is this? Are you planning an ambush? I can see 270 degrees around me you know.

Or am I supposed to go 'Yes' and then you go 'Well have it alone, you bug-eyed freak'?

Laura

On Wednesday at 12:18 Martin replied:

And they all say I'm the paranoid one.

No, I'm not going to ambush you. No one else wants to talk to me 'cos they think I'm a dick for being horrible about you.

But quite apart from that I am genuinely sorry.

On Wednesday at 12:20 Laura replied:

Are you sorry because you were incredibly hurtful (and untruthful), or because you don't want me to write any more stuff about you online?

On Wednesday at 12:24 Martin replied:

Bit of both. Which comments were yours at www.yourtheatre.
com? I'll tell you which were mine...

P.S. How am I doing in the poll?

On Wednesday at 12:28 Laura wrote:

Let's put it this way. You've pulled ahead of Gwyn, due to a
suspicious number of votes from one 'Johannes Jester'. However,
the poll is far from closed.
Good weekend?

On Wednesday at 12:34 Martin replied:

I've had better.

P.S. I'm not taking it back about Acklington Stanley, though.
They really do stink.

Part Nine
Pirates

The Stag Night · Captain Claw
Sad News for Acklington Stanley
Words of Warning

Stag Night

Hi, Martin,

I didn't want to call too early because I guessed you might be having a 'lie-in' today. How was the stag night? Hope it went OK – no need to give me all the gory details. Lovely weather for the boat trip. I trust you all behaved yourself.

    Lots of love,

Mum

On Sunday at 13:45 Martin wrote:

Hullo the mater

It all started so well. We had a bottle of champagne and went along the Thames, and it was a very nice evening. Bit fuzzy about some of the details, but I'll put it together as best I can.

We were all joking away and teasing Chris about tying him to things, setting him up with a ladyboy, jesting about having a hangover the next day, standard pleasantries. It was great to see everyone. Really nice atmosphere.

But as we passed Blackfriars Bridge a sudden and very local fog descended. Strange noises arose all around us, laughter and what sounded like the clink of metal on metal - swords or perhaps loose change.

'Look!' Barney shouted, and he pointed at a pair of tattered black sails suddenly looming out of the fog. Almost before he'd finished speaking he fell, shot through the neck with an antique pistol.

The tour-guide was the next to go, cut from one end to the

other with a rusty cutlass.

Out of the mist more strange figures appeared, some with hooks, some with parrots, some with eyepatches. We were surrounded. Then a tall figure stepped forth, with a polka-dot headscarf and a wooden leg.

'It's your choice, mateys,' he said 'Join me crew or I'll keel-haul ya.'

I stepped forward and shouted, 'I'd rather die than serve you, Captain Claw,' which was when someone bludgeoned me from behind.

At least, that's how I remember it. Certainly explains why my head aches and I have a tattoo of a mermaid on my arm this morning. Then I woke up back at the flat. I thought it was all a dream before I saw the note on the table: 'If you want to see Chris again send 50,000 Gold Doubloons to Captain Claw, c/o Mrs Claw, Spooky Skull Island, the Sea.'

Other than that the evening was fairly uneventful. Tried ringing earlier but I guess you were having lunch in the garden.
Lots of Love
Martin

P.S. I don't really have a tattoo of a mermaid on my arm.
P.P.S. It's on my arse.

On Sunday at 14:32 Emily wrote:

Martin,
Hope you enjoyed the stag. Writing to check Chris didn't get up to any mischief. I will know if you are lying because I have asked more than one person to see if you can keep your stories straight. Mike has already sold you out, and Barney is in the next room tied to a chair and about to crack. So you may as well tell me everything and save your own skin.
Lots of love
Look forward to seeing your tattoo at the Wedding,
          Emily

PS. As long as the tattoo's on your arm, that is.

On Sunday at 14:45 Emily wrote:

Dear Stag-Nighters,

Thanks for your candid replies. Your stories check out and Chris is off the hook.

Wait a minute ...

I thought he was in bed. But there's only a note from someone called Captain Claw ... Wonder how he holds a pen with two hooks for hands? (Only Barney noticed that about him. Surprisingly no one else mentioned it).

If you jokers think I'd pay 50,000 doubloons to get Chris back you have another think coming.

I can't believe you all collaborated to provide a cover story ...

Lots of love,

Emily

PS. Chris cracked and told me the whole sordid tale. He would have made a rubbish pirate.

On Sunday at 14:50 Mike wrote:

Good going, Barney. You blew the whole story. We told you to stick to the facts we all agreed.

Captain Claw has two *eye-patches*, not *hooks*.

Likewise I don't remember anyone mentioning anything about any *Admiral* Martin. And that bit about you and Mrs Claw was sheer fantasy.

Still, Emily has only penetrated the *first* cover-story. Hopefully the robot Chris is going to last till the wedding, and the real Chris should be on the beach in Buenos Aires with that barmaid by now ...

On Sunday at 14:51 Mike wrote:

Oops, didn't mean to reply to all with that email. Hope Emily doesn't read it.

Lucky I didn't mention the Polish lap-dancer.

On Sunday at 14:53 Mike wrote:

Oops again. Sorry, Chris.

On Sunday at 15:00 Martin wrote:

I've reread the wedding schedule. What's this? DJ Claw? Hooks for hands and they'd still rather he played than DJ Idiot?

Sweet Thames, Run Softly

All right, Prickles,

How was the stag? Let me make myself very clear: I don't want to read a fucking word about pirates.

Ella

On Sunday at 18:12 Martin replied:

OK OK. Or should that be 'Aye aye, Captain Ella'?

Actually the boat trip was a bit bizarre even without pirates. Although don't tell the others I revealed that there weren't any.

Surprisingly we were the only stag-night boat trip, and we were up topside with two Canadian Goths and their parents, a group of Japanese pensioners, some giggly Italian teenagers, and the tour guide. Of all of them, I think the tour guide knew the least about London. Not just nothing, less than nothing.

I quote: 'All right, everyone speak English?... OK, you won't understand a word I'm saying, but hardly anyone does anyway, so I'll keep going... Sometimes people have a problem understanding my accent. Anyone having any difficulties? [*a forest of hands goes up, including Chris's*]. Well I was born with it and I can't change it now... Right, up ahead we're coming up to London Bridge [*we were approaching Vauxhall Bridge, but anyway*]... The story is some dumb Yank bought that, thinking it was Tower Bridge, which we'll see in a minute [*much laughter from the Canadians and others unaware that they are going under Vauxhall Bridge*]... On your left that's the Houses of Parliament. Not sure what they do in there but they get paid a lot to sit

315

around and do it... And that on your left is the London Eye. It's actually a huge windmill that raises and lowers Tower Bridge [*lots of oohs and aahs*]... Only joking [*some very disappointed looks*]. I tell you if you ever go on a date with a London girl, offer to take her up the London Eye [*some ribaldry at the back of the boat ensues. A boatswain is detached to come up and stand next to us disapprovingly*]... Now, where were we? [*Chris: 'You tell us, mate, you're the tour guide'*]...Oh, here's the Embankment. If you look closely you can see Terry and Julie crossing over the river [*baffled silence*]. Nah, that one never works. You all right love? I wasn't sure whether you were dropping off... This is Blackfriars Bridge, and anyone who had breakfast at the café over there can tell you why that is... Do wave to the people, otherwise they tend to drop bricks on us, or worse. Don't look so worried, sir. It hardly ever happens... On your right now is the Tate Modern. For those of you who don't know English, that's pronounced with a silent "e"... This is the Millennium Bridge, otherwise known as the wobbly bridge, built, as you can tell from the name, over one thousand years ago... Bloody hell, that was a bit close. [*Seagull nearly smacks into guide, to much applause. And not only from us*]... Wave at the people on this bridge now, otherwise they'll think we're being rude [*What they think of us is not clear, as it is a gang of youths who start gobbing down on us. Wisely, several people put up umbrellas or pull up hoods. Barney, unwisely, looks up with his mouth open.*] Little fuckers... Sorry about that, ladies and gentlemen, and please pardon my French... No, love, I don't actually speak French. It was a figure of speech... And coming up now is the famous Tower of London, where the Queen lives. Looks very old, doesn't it? In fact it was built last year...'

There were no pirates, but there was bloody nearly a mutiny.

We had to wait for ages for taxis on to the restaurant, but when we left the Japanese group were still pointing at the Tower of London and bickering, while the Goth teens looked as if they were considering suicide. Even more than Goth teens usually do. Felt bloody proud to be a Londoner after that little display, I can tell you. Didn't tip, and got cussed as a result. Presumably somewhere someone who actually knows and likes London is bound and gagged in a cupboard with a tour guide hat on.

How was the bachelorette thing?

On Sunday at 18:40 Ella replied:

None of your business.

You see, we all agreed to say that. Rather than spending the whole night making up a story about pirates ...

Re: Re: Re: Re: Acklington Stanley

You'll be glad to hear Acklington Stanley broke up. Jez the drummer quit. Or rather, he didn't turn up at the show and when they phoned his folks he'd gone travelling in Bolivia for six months.

I took some of the more offensive stuff off the blog over the weekend. As you'll no doubt have noticed. Mostly the bits about your friends and your hairy hands. Ross threatened to sue. In relation to the bits about his bedroom and speculating where he spends his time, rather than the hairy hands, I should make clear. Oh yeah, he says you need to get milk.

The poll is closed. Sorry to tell you, but you didn't win.

On Monday at 9:40 Martin wrote:

Very surprised to hear that about Jez. I guess they really were a band that was going places.

I'm not at all gloating that the Stanley have split. Not only is it always good for people to express themselves, but in my living room I have a thousand badges saying 'Acklington Stanley Should Shut the Fuck Up' that I had printed and are now entirely useless.

So I guess Gwyn was cheered up by the poll result? These things only mean anything when they're voted for by 'the kids', after all...
Martin

P.S. Sod the hairy hands. Take back the accusation that I am a 'wannabe' hipster. I didn't sit through all those Belgian movies

318

and avant-industrial gigs to be labelled a wannabe. I once had a
pee in the ICA next to Steve Mackay. I was showing everyone
the splash-stain on my right trainer for weeks. And I know DJ
Idiot. So there.

P.P.S. I spotted Victor Lewis-Smith rooting through a bin in Soho
once, and wrote in to *Heat*. Although they didn't print it. And
come to think of it it may have been a tramp.

On Monday at 9:43 Laura replied:

Have you not seen the poll? There was a late surge in favour
of a third option: 'Die alone before considering dating either
of these buffoons.' Oh well. Gwyn suspects the interference of
disgruntled Fork fans.

On Monday at 9:47 Martin replied:

Well, they're probably right. About the best option for you,
I mean, not about wanting to hear more from Fork. How is he
taking the break-up?

On Monday at 9:53 Laura replied:

Which one?

On Monday at 9:55 Martin replied:

Sorry?

On Monday at 9:57 Laura replied:

I thought you were referring to my chucking Gwyn out over

the weekend. He's staying with his mum.

On Monday at 10:03 Martin replied:

But surely the poll results weren't in by then?

On Monday at 10:06 Laura replied:

Martin, I don't run my life according to what a bunch of freaks on the internet think. The poll was only meant to be a joke. There was no need to spend the whole week voting under a series of increasingly ludicrous pseudonyms.

On Monday at 10:08 Martin replied:

'Ludicrous pseudonyms'? I think Robusto P. Rickles and D. Umpgwyn would be very upset to hear you say that. So why did you ditch him?

On Monday at 10:13 Laura replied:

Acklington Stanley really were shit, weren't they? And besides, he's fucking fat.

On Monday at 10:15 Martin replied:

I don't suppose this means there's any chance…?

On Monday at 10:18 Laura replied:

I don't think so, baldy.

Kate Staple

On Monday at 11:23 Martin wrote:

I've seen Martin Sergeant and he doesn't look too happy. I take it his holiday with Kate didn't rekindle the old spark?

On Monday at 11:30 Barney replied:

Yeah, it's turned out great. She got back last night and came straight over to mine. Couldn't have planned it better. They spent the whole week in bed.
Barney

On Monday at 11:33 Martin replied:

OK, I've missed something. Reread what you wrote to me, and then send me some sense.

On Monday at 11:40 Barney replied:

I meant exactly what I wrote. They both got food poisoning on the first night. I'm over the moon.
By the way, I've got some pretty blurry memories of the stag. Were we really kidnapped by pirates?

On Monday at 11:41 Barney wrote:

By the way, that was a joke.

On Monday at 11:45 Martin replied:

Barney, sometimes I wish you had been...
Glad to hear Kate was sick. Which is a pretty sick sentiment in itself, but you know what I mean.
Gotta go and jerk Martin around.

On Monday at 11:46 Martin wrote:

Just reread that, and realised it was open to misinterpretation. I meant:
I have to go and ask Martin Sergeant about his holiday. Did he bring back souvenirs, I wonder, or a series of labelled sick-bags?

Wedding

On Friday at 12:32 Sally wrote:

Hi Martin,
Tried my dress on last night and it looks absolutely stunning.
Weather forecast looks all right. It should be a really great day.
Enough small talk.
I'm writing to check you're not going to pull anything stupid
at the wedding tomorrow. No sock, no drunken rants, no
weeping, no dancing on the tables (unless other people are doing
it, and even then not during the actual ceremony). OK?
Look forward to seeing you tomorrow,
Sally

PS - Sorry to hear about the poll.

On Friday at 12:40 Martin wrote:

I promise I won't do anything to spoil Chris and Emily's
special day. Jesus, what do you take me for?
*stops stencilling 'Sally is a cheating hairbrush' on back of
dinner jacket*

On Friday at 12:43 Sally replied:

Uncross your fingers.

On Friday at 12:45 Martin replied:

OK, they're uncrossed. I promise.

On Friday at 12:50 Sally wrote:

And please persuade Barney not to dress as a pirate ...

On Friday at 12:51 Martin replied:

Oh, but he looks so cute.

I wanted him to leap out from behind the altar waving his cutlass when the vicar asks if anyone knows any reason why these two cannot be lawfully joined, then shouting: 'Aarrgh, I know a reason! He's signed up to be my cabin boy in a contract written in blood.'

It would certainly make it a day never to forget.

On Friday at 12:55 Sally replied:

You know of course that Emily's dad is a farmer, and has access to firearms ...

On Friday at 13:01 Martin replied:

I'll have a quiet word with Barney...

A Word of Advice

On Friday at 14:24 Emily wrote:

Hi Martin,

I hope the weather stays nice for tomorrow. We've had the rehearsal and everything went great. The vicar doesn't stutter, the ringbearer has been warned not to eat the ring accidentally (as has Barney), Chris hasn't seen the dress, my uncle hasn't got the best man drunk, our parents aren't engaged in an increasingly elaborate series of misunderstandings, there are no senile but heart-warming aged relatives causing genial chaos, no one has accidentally told my father I'm pregnant (I'm not), and Chris assures me he is neither having last-minute cold feet nor hiding a secret room full of dead ex-wives. According to my extensive research that just about covers everything that can go wrong at a wedding. Except for one thing.

Martin, I swear to God if you fuck things up I will kill you. You will be the first man ever to be beaten to death with a bouquet. Try to pretend for one day that Chris and I are the centre of attention, rather than mere pawns in your own convoluted psychodrama. Try to imagine that when I look back at my wedding day in fifty years' time, I hope my chief memory will not be you wrestling naked with my father, you swinging Sally off on a chandelier, or you falling into the wedding cake. In fact, if I may be blunt, I hope my memories of this momentous day will hardly feature you at all.

Look forward to seeing you.

Love,

Emily

PS. And I'm holding you personally responsible for Barney as well. If he has as much as an eyepatch or a parrot with him I'll keel-haul you both myself.

PPS. I'm not joking.

Part Ten
The Next Big Thing

The Wedding

The Sunday Times Style
Supplement

Departures • Big Dreams

The End

Re: Wedding

Hi, everyone,

Excuse the group email. This is a quick note to say thanks for coming and making it such a special day for both of us. In particular I'd like to thank Mike for being an excellent best man, Emily would like to thank Ella for making such a lovely bridesmaid, and we'd both like to thank Barney for not coming dressed as a pirate. (Those who know Barney will understand, those who don't have a lot to be grateful for). Look forward to seeing you all when we get back from Sardinia. Be good to each other, and to yourselves.

Mr and Mrs Chris and Emily Fence

On Sunday at 15:01 Mike replied:

Chris and Emily,

It's your honeymoon! Stop bloody emailing and start producing little Fences. So I see Emily has taken your surname?

Congratulations, guys,

Mike

On Sunday at 15:04 Emily replied:

It's under discussion. Christ, you'd think after 26 years of being a farmer's daughter called Emily Lamb I'd be glad to change, but no, I have to fall in love with a Fence ...

On Sunday at 15:06 Barney replied:

Sounds painful! *joke*

On Sunday at 15:08 Ella wrote:

Barney, we have to have a serious talk about this comedy thing. No joke.

Re: Re: Wedding

Hi, Martin,

Hope you didn't make a complete flaming tit of yourself at the wedding!

So tell me, without mentioning pirates once:

What was the Bride's dress like? Was she pretty?

What was her mother like?

Did you smooch a bridesmaid?

Did you smooch Sally?

Did ya cry?

Have you seen the papers today?

Who caught the bouquet?

Lots of love,

Lucy

PS: Lady came through all clear at the vet yesterday. In case you were worrying about it during the wedding.

On Sunday at 15:10 Martin replied:

Hi Lucy

Glad to hear about Lady. No, I didn't make a flaming tit of myself. Not completely. In fact, apart from dancing badly and falling over due to slippery shoes, then insisting on showing everyone my shoes and how slippery they were to prove I wasn't drunk, I was perfectly behaved. Although a bit drunk.

Yes, the bride was gorgeous, and from the looks of her mother, she'll age gracefully.

Her dress? It was white. It was a dress. There was a floaty bit and a shiny bit. It was nice.

I was dancing with a bridesmaid when I had the shoe malfunction. You may be surprised to learn there was no smooching.

Didn't smooch Sally either. It was cool. We had a nice chat about her catching the bouquet. Despite a desperate dive to avoid it. I didn't cry, even at that. Although there was something stuck behind one of my contact lenses at one point. Properly. Ah, why would you believe me when no one else does?

I liked the way you snuck the papers in there. Yes, I saw the piece you are referring to.

I'm absolutely ecstatic about it.

Lots of Love

Martin

P.S. To add to my good mood: best man he may have been, but Mike dances like a monkey being teased with a sharp stick. Several sharp sticks, to be exact.

On Sunday at 15:15 Lucy replied:

By 'ecstatic' do you mean 'flabbergasted and planning revenge'? I don't get it. Are we talking about the same thing? I mean the bit in *Style* where they name David Fauntleroy as their 'Next Big Thing'? You're not a teensy bit upset? That's pretty big of you.

On Sunday at 15:17 Martin replied:

My dear Lucy

Let me reassure you I am as bitter and small a person as I have ever been. I am thrilled because being named the *Sunday Times*'s next big thing is as brutal a kiss of death as putting a gun in your mouth and propelling your tonsils through the back of your head. In fact, the latter is almost always preferable, at least in career terms. Remember those posh rockers who were going to be huge? The bloke who was filming a version of *Ulysses* set in downtown Manhattan? That comedy double-act who used to sing at Elton's parties? No? Not even I can remember the names of any of them. Yes, I can, the band was called the Double-Barrels. Being Style's 'Next Big Thing' is the next worst thing to Michael Stipe declaring he likes your band. Concrete Blonde, anyone? Seriously, anyone for Grant Lee Buffalo?

That article is the best news I've heard all year. All at once the world seems to make sense again. And the picture of David is rubbish. Even photographed down a dark stairwell and dressed in black he looks like a good luck troll.

I am utterly jubilant.

Dreams

On Sunday at 15:20 Martin wrote:

Dear Sally
See? I told you I could behave.
I saw the piece on David in the paper. That's great. I'm
genuinely pleased for you. So you guys are leaving London?
Lots of Love
Martin

On Sunday at 15:57 Sally wrote:

Hi, Martin,
Yes, it's official. I've got some work at a theatre in Bristol and
David's coming with me to finish his new play. It's going to be
really exciting. Thanks for saying about the paper, that's sweet of
you.
I've been thinking about what you asked me at the wedding, if
you still want to know the answer.
Lots of love
Sally

On Sunday at 16:04 Martin replied:

Sally, I think we've left it a bit late to do 'the Timewarp' now.
But leaving London? I know, there's the dirty pigeons, and
you can never get a proper taxi on a Saturday night, and it's
expensive, and it's full of fakes and freaks, and it's dangerous,
and the weather's shit, and the public transport is a joke, and

everyone hates Londoners, and the streets are full of drunks, and there's the constant threat of crime, and no one smiles or says hello, and it's polluted and...

I lost my train of thought. Go on.

On Sunday at 16:08 Sally replied:

I meant when you asked what I'd change about you if there was one thing.

On Sunday at 16:11 Martin replied:

OK, OK, I'm doing something about the hands. Was it that?

On Sunday at 16:14 Sally replied:

Well, there was that. But I thought, actually, people don't ever change. And probably the things that made it so we didn't work out are exactly what someone else will fall in love with you for.

On Sunday at 16:17 Martin replied:

That's so beautiful.
But seriously, you took 24 hours to come up with that?
How was David about the bouquet thing?

On Sunday at 16:25 Sally replied:

Freaked. But tell me honestly, is David really a total wanker?

On Sunday at 16:27 Martin replied:

Well, he can't change if he is.

On Sunday at 16:35 Sally replied:

Maybe people can change. That was quite diplomatic.
So what is next for Martin Sargent?

On Sunday at 16:40 Martin replied:

What, after storming around my room shouting, 'David is a
wanker. David is a wanker'? Again. Possibly one of the reasons
Ross is moving out. I quote: 'Among other things, I want to
experiment living somewhere nice with someone nice.' Trying
not to take it personally.

On Sunday at 16:43 Sally replied:

Or maybe people can't change after all.

On Sunday at 16:45 Martin replied:

Let me tell you, Sally, I have dreams too. Big dreams. I'm not
going to work in that office for ever. Might go travelling for a
year. Maybe do teacher training.

P.S. If you are moving, can I have that book about Jesus back?
My mum keeps asking if I've read it.

Felicitations

On Friday at 11:02 Martin wrote:

Hey Emily

Hope the honeymoon was great. Thanks so much for inviting me to the wedding. It really got me thinking, you know, about love. I guess you heard that Sally's moving down to Bristol. I'm pleased for her. David too, I guess. Did you know it's one of the rainiest cities in Britain? Anyway, I suppose there's not much chance of me and Sally getting back together now. Things are still pretty odd with Laura, too. She's having some time alone. As I guess am I, but she seems to be doing so intentionally. Or at least so her website claims. We aren't speaking that much.

Ross moved out at the weekend. He assures me it's not entirely personal. He's decided to go travelling for a few months, and he's living at home for a bit to save money. He wants to take a break from his job, and I think he's decided that the world isn't quite ready yet for a sitcom that juxtaposes the romantic pratfalls and misadventures of a bunch of eccentric but loveable characters sharing a house in London and a scathing critique of the machinations of global capitalism. He left a bottle of milk, which was sweet of him. I suppose the next couple of months will give me a chance to think about what I really want, and to try and discover who the real Martin Sargent is. Maybe it's time for a change of career. Hope I didn't spoil your big day.
Lots of Love
Martin

Hey Martin,

A change of career sounds exciting. Although Chris and I were talking the other day and we realised we've never been entirely sure what it is that you actually do now.

The honeymoon was amazing, although of course we missed you. Seriously, thanks for coming to the wedding. It was great to have you there, and thank you again for behaving yourself. Although we still haven't got to the bottom of who it was who asked Auntie Claire if she'd ever noticed that her baby girl looks like 'the young Mussolini'. She hadn't in fact noticed, although it certainly does. It's the big bald head, I think, rather than a penchant for giving long dramatic speeches in Italian and making trains run on time. We suspect the culprit was also responsible for persuading Barney to eat the pot-pourri at the hotel. He was very disappointed when Chris told him there's no such thing as 'edible confetti from Japan'.

Yes, I suppose it is unlikely you'll get back with Sally now. Although I can't say I ever thought it was hugely likely. To be perfectly honest neither Chris nor I could quite work out what she saw in you. I had a theory, but Ella dismissed it. 'Rock and Roll Heart' is rubbish. And besides, Chris has it on tape. For obvious reasons.

Are you sure you want to discover the real Martin Sargent? Oh, and of course you won't be entirely alone ...

Emily X

On Friday at 11:20 Martin replied:

Aargh, so you know about that. Yeah, I had a sudden and surprising access of affection for Barney during the reception, and I knew he wanted to change where he was living. I almost instantly regretted it, of course. I think I realised what I'd done when he said 'And I can set my decks up in the living room.' No, it was probably a little later, when he suggested we give one day

each week a costumed theme. Well, I suppose I did always want a pet when I was a kid. I must remember to keep the lid down on the loo. On the plus side, I've always wanted to meet Kate Staple. I hear such astonishing things about her.
Martin

P.S. Now I think of it, I was wondering if you could let me have Felicity's number? The cute bridesmaid? We were dancing to ABC and I think I was getting the look of love from her a bit. Until I fell on my arse.

On Friday at 11:32 Emily replied:

Ah, Martin, maybe one day you'll find true love.

Heavens above! It may indeed have been the look of love that Felicity was giving you, although she did tell me later she was having trouble with a contact lens (and by the way no one was fooled by your pathetic excuse for blubbing all the way through the readings). She also commented that she's never seen dancing like yours before. Take that as you will. She didn't tell me not to give you her number, so that's a pretty promising start by your standards. But seriously, mate, have you ever thought of just getting a hobby?

Or is the message of all this that while lovers come and go, mates last for ever?

I'll text you Felicity's number, if you really want it. But before I do, I should probably check you know that Felicity is sixteen years old. How about I give you her number and you call her in a few years' time when the age difference is a little more appropriate?

Furthermore, I'm a little surprised that you would be interested in following that up, considering the cosy little tête-à-tête you and Ella were having at the reception. What was that all about?

On Friday at 11:35 Martin replied:

Hey Emily

Thanks for letting me know about Felicity. It probably would have been kinder to mention her age before you got my hopes up, but anyway... I think on reflection I'll leave it. I'm always available to babysit, though. Not in a creepy way. Crikey, she's very well-developed for sixteen. I simply mean that as a compliment.

Now you mention it, I did have a fairly long chat with Ella. To be honest I'm pretty hazy on most of the details, but I do seem to recall suggesting that if we're both still single at thirty we should get married, for the presents. It seemed like a pretty good idea at the time. That said, I believe we also agreed to go halves on a racehorse.

On Friday at 11:40 Emily replied:

Thirty? I hate to point it out, but that doesn't leave you much wiggle-room ...

PS. 'Well-developed'? Stop digging, Martin. I know exactly how you mean that.

On Friday at 11:43 Martin replied:

Thanks for the crack about my age. Jeez, Emily, I'm only 25. Even if my hairline does seem to be taking early retirement.

Now, I know this is a little premature, but if you and Chris are planning on having kids, I'm very much available for godfathering duties. No pressure, but I thought I'd get in there with the offer before Mike does.

Oh, since you asked: the message I'm drawing from the past couple of months is this: if you systematically make a prick of yourself, you end up living with an idiot. By the way, Barney wanted me to ask you (and Chris) to dinner on Tuesday. We hope you can come.

It's Pirates Night.

Re: Just a Pint

On Friday at 12:00 Ella wrote:

> Hallo, Sargent
> How are you doing? Still feel a little weepy?

On Friday at 12:03 Martin replied:

> How many times? I. Had. Something. In. My. Eye.

On Friday at 12:04 Ella replied:

> Yes, I know that. A load of tears. Anyway, enough badinage. What about this pint you keep promising me? How are you fixed for this evening?

On Friday at 12:07 Martin replied:

> Tonight I'm free. And God knows I'll be ready for a drink by then. So that sounds perfect.

On Friday at 12:13 Ella replied:

> Great. I assume Felicity has homework to do.

[handwritten margin note:] bandinge 342 presumably this is mea as bandy - not to ban words. (NOT IN DICTIONARY).

On Friday at 12:15 Martin replied:

Emily had stern words for me on the topic of Felicity. I swear I never would have guessed her age. I've decided not to pursue it any further, and I'm very much regretting having used my work computer to google her earlier in the week.

On Friday at 12:18 Ella replied:

To clear the air, I take it you've forgotten our conversation at the reception.

On Friday at 12:21 Martin replied:

I'm afraid I'm drawing a total blank on it.

On Friday at 12:25 Ella replied:

Me too. I'm glad we understand one another. See you later on. I'll give you a ring when I've decided where we're going.

On Friday at 12:31 Martin replied:

Can I make a suggestion? There's a haunted pub in Newgate Street I've always wanted to check out. Apparently there's a grey monk who lurks around the men's loos and moans ominously. They've also got a good range of regional ales, I'm told.

P.S. I assume that among the things we aren't remembering is your promise to marry me in five years? For the presents, obviously.
P.P.S. Not that I necessarily think there's anything wrong with having a five-year plan...

On Friday at 12:36 Ella replied:

Thanks for your suggestion, Sargent. I think you've illustrated exactly why I'll be the one choosing the venue.

PS Bingo. To clarify the terms of our pact, it only holds if no one better comes along before then. And that's a way scarier thought than a haunted toilet. Looking on the bright side, the world may have ended before then.

I'd also like to remind you that thirty was a compromise figure: you suggested right away, I said sixty. Not that I can remember actually agreeing to this deal. Verbal contract, mate. It's not worth the paper it's written on.

PPS Now I think about it, though, I do recall you repeatedly requesting 'a go' wearing my bridesmaid's dress …

PPPS What the hell? Five-year plan? You're taking your love-life advice from Josef Stalin now?

On Friday at 12:43 Martin replied:

What can I say? Mass-murdering tyrant he may have been, but who else's advice am I going to take? Barney's? He mentioned to me the other day that sometimes he likes to practise DJing in the nude. But then I expect you knew that. As if I needed another reason to dread living with him. I still can't figure out what you saw in the guy. However, since his decks are set up in our living room, I may be about to find out.

By the way, if you ever mention the dress thing in public I solemnly swear I'm going to hold you to our little agreement. Verbal contract or no.

See you later, Ms Tvertko.

P.S. Just a thought, but wouldn't it be funny if after all this we ended up together?

On Friday at 12:45 Ella replied:

Don't count your chickens, Sargent. It's amazing how much
more appealing the thought of ending up with you makes the
prospect of dying alone. No offence. I should also mention I'm
having serious second thoughts about the racehorse.

On Friday at 12:47 Martin replied:

Oh, Ella, always trying to get round me with your sweet-talk.
I think we both know I wasn't the only one with something in
my eye at the wedding. Could it be that underneath that frosty
façade, a tender heart waits to be thawed?

On Friday at 12:50 Ella replied:

You're completely right. Martin, it's always been you. Oh how
long these nights have been ...
   Wouldn't that be a happy ending to your sad little tale, if it were
true? Unfortunately, though, it's not. People often seem to assume
that because I seem cold and sarcastic, I have a problem expressing
how I really feel. Let me warn you right know that would be a
grievous mistake to make. If I was getting a bit dewy-eyed, it was
because those stupid bridesmaid's shoes were killing my feet. Actually,
my heart is considerably frostier than my façade would suggest.
   On the other hand, there's something about a man dressed as
a pirate ...

On Friday at 12:52 Martin wrote:

Hey Barney
This may sound weird, but I'm going to need to borrow a
bandanna ...
